DEDICATION

For Kathy and Diane — without their unremitting support and love, this book could not have been accomplished — and for Oprah, Eloise, Margo, and Bettina — with eternal love and appreciation.

Maui Whispers

RICK OLSON

For Jim & Marguerite
Best Friends!
With Aloha!

DOUBLEBOW BOOKS

Maui, Hawaii

Website: www.mauibooks.com
E-mail: islander@maui.net
Phone/Fax: (808) 874-6724

Published by

DOUBLEBOW BOOKS
P.O. Box 2343
Kihei, Hawaii 96753 USA

TO ORDER COPIES of *Maui Whispers*:

Website: www.mauibooks.com
E-mail: islander@maui.net
Phone/Fax: 808-874-6724

This is a work of fiction. The names and characters portrayed are the work of the author's imagination. Any resemblance to actual persons, either living or dead, is purely coincidental.

ISBN: 0-975-91320-4
SAN: 256-114X
LCCN: 2004095446

Photo Cover by David Olsen Photography
Cover Design by Adam Carbajal of SpectraColor
Hawai'i

ACKNOWLEDGMENTS

A heartfelt mahalo goes to Adam, Victor, David, Pelenise, Janet, and Bruddah Tom for their care and expertise.

A special thanks to Paul Thoreaux, whose gift of portraying the peculiarities of folks along his journeys inspired me to travel the world and finally sit down and write.

Lastly, eternal gratitude to everyone who encouraged me to write this story, and to the islanders of Maui for their precious spirit of aloha that made it easy to fall in love with an extraordinary paradise.

CONTENTS

SPRING

SUMMER

FALL

WINTER

SKY

Bewildered by the sudden turn of events, Sky Shafer charged through the dangerous lava tube in hellbent pursuit. The curse of his gimpy leg fueled a rising anger. His prisoner had bolted.

Directly ahead, a long, phallic-shaped stalactite descended from the ceiling, cloaked in decades of darkness. Sky's powerful halogen shot flickers of light all over the pitch-black cave — yet failed to illuminate the well-hung protrusion in time. The lurking lavacicle pricked his head as his momentum sent it crashing to the floor. Oh no — not another scar, he thought. Wait until I get ahold of that little punk.

"Come back, damn it!" he yelled at the fleeing escapee.

In response, the 19-year-old prisoner let loose a taunting, high-pitched scream "eeeee-aaaaa!" which echoed through the black tunnel.

Boomer had carefully planned his escape. Short, cunning, and familiar with the twists and turns of the mile-long lava tube, the redheaded spelunker held the advantage. Scrambling through tiny passageways and scurrying over piles of rocks, he darted along the footpath of crushed cinder like a startled gecko.

The tunnel widened, and the spotlight strapped to his head scanned an enormous volcanic room. An eerie, shimmering glow spilled down his narrow face — revealing an ear-to-ear smile.

Sky was also familiar with this Hana cave, but at the age of 46, a couple inches above six feet, and hindered by a limp, he was hard put to capture his wily ward. A minute ago, he believed he had bonded with the convicted thief. Now he was frustrated, exhausted, and tasting his own blood. In the distance the darting light grew fainter. The tunnel quieted. Heavy breathing and the painful thumping of his heart pummeled the silence. Adding to his own labored drumbeats was a disturbing notion that he was left alone in a cave littered with ghostly legends.

"Hey, thought we were friends..." he yelled into the black void. "Damn it, you're out in a week. Don't blow it now!"

He stumbled over a pile of beer cans and broken stalagmite. Entombed by the crisp, dry climate, the empty cans were perfectly preserved. Some of the larger piles concealed small bits of bone fragments — animal and human remains.

The vertical escape shaft was fast approaching and, once outside, the prisoner could slip into the remote jungle area of East Maui.

"Boomer... let's talk," he pleaded. Then to himself, *I should quit working with these ungrateful....*

Once a month, Sky volunteered for a community program that mentored model prisoners for early release. He gave his protégé the choice of hiking, paddling, or exploring caves. The following day he usually introduced his ward to a few potential employers.

Rounding the last bend, Sky saw the shaft of light blazing down the rough, wooden steps. The exit was empty and painfully silent. He should have trusted me, he thought. Can't he tell I'm an ex-con?

Knowing that the chase was over, he slowed to a walk and approached the exit halfheartedly. It would be difficult returning to Wailuku and explaining the escape, especially as Boomer had been an exceptional prisoner and a favorite of the warden. Maybe he needed to rethink his volunteer role with these unpredictable felons.

Sky caught his breath and looked up the steep hole toward daylight. On the rim of the entrance, Boomer's mischievous-looking baby blues were staring back. A sharp sun spotlighted three auburn whiskers on his pointed chin, while a tattooed gecko played on his bony wrist.

"Thought you was a caver, Mr. Shafer," he teased. "Hope you got a little ole band-aid for yer head."

"Get down here, you skinny little runt. What the hell was that all about?"

"Oh man, I was, like, jus' messin' with ya. I always race with my buds here. Come on man, let's go back and, like check out some more tunnels."

"Well... I'm not a damn teenager, you know. I'm just trying to help, and you're not making it easy."

"Sorry, Sky. Think you can squeeze through that small tube at the end of the rear fork?"

"Try me. Just don't squirm away too fast with that skinny ass of yours."

Sky knew that he could worm his way through most small places, but sometimes his muscular chest and arms jammed, largely due to three years of weight lifting in the penitentiary. Prison was 20 years ago, but his upper body still had the wedge shape of a champion swimmer. Although the shape was nicely suited for the beach, in tight underground passages it was a distinct liability.

Before climbing back down, Boomer filled his lungs with the thick, perfumed air of the lush, tropical landscape. Gentle breezes caressed his senses with warm, pungent aromas, sweetened from a pre-dawn rain. By the time Boomer was halfway to the floor, the air turned cool and still.

They passed endless side tunnels, where not even cockroaches dared to enter. A thousand years ago, 2100-degree molten lava oozed down the slopes of Haleakala, blistered a path to the sea, crusted over, and formed the underground tubes.

Entering a side lava tube, they walked over a floor that looked like the whipped-up swirls of chocolate frosting on a cake. Soon their lights revealed an entire room that appeared to be wrapped in "Willy Wonka" shades of chocolate. The ceiling dripped with fudge-covered stalactites, and the walls were riddled with lava spikes, softened by a creamy brown coating. At the far end, they dropped to their bellies and crawled 30 feet through an 18-inch high passage, before finding a small cavern.

Once inside, Sky noticed that the large cracks, running down the grey walls, were outlined in red from earlier steam vents. He shivered at the thought of steam pouring into this claustrophobic cavern. A basalt boulder rested nearby, loaded with colorful minerals. The world-renowned sea-life artist made a mental note to let the vibrant reds, blues, and golds inspire his next creative project.

A towering, rickety, wood ladder leaned against the far wall. The narrow structure discouraged access to anything larger than a beady-eyed rat, but a black hole above the top rung tantalized the curiosities of the intrepid trailblazers.

"I should stick you in there for a couple of hours without a torch, so you can think about your future," taunted Sky with an unseen smile.

"Hey, man, I'll go, but I'm taking my damn light so I don't freak. I can deal with tight places, but not in the dark. You're an ex-con — you should know."

"Don't worry," Sky replied, feeling a kindred connection now that Boomer had unshackled his secret past. "Trust me. I'll have a backup light behind you."

Strange words coming from me, Sky thought, realizing he hadn't completely trusted anyone since his release from the lockup all those years ago. He thought about the past women in his life and wondered if that's why his relationships always failed — maybe there was a reason he couldn't trust some of them; and maybe he was the one — the one who never allowed himself to be trusted by someone special. Then he thought about how it might be different with the new lady in his life. She was clearly unlike the others.

"Come on, Sky, there's a huge room ahead! Hurry up man!" yelled the redhead, returning to his boyish enthusiasm.

"Right behind you, pal," Sky answered, feeling good again about the unspoken bond that had been developed over the last few hours. This kid might turn out OK.

BEACHED PYGMY

Rosie Faber screamed, and gasped for air. She was being buried alive in a large sandy mound on a remote Maui beach. There were two men involved, maybe more.

Her heaving slowed and her wailing grew fainter as she heard chirping overhead. The digital chirping sounded soft, but incessant, and as she snapped out of her nightmare she knew it was the sound of trouble. And trouble never rang at a convenient time.

Bright-red signals blinked from the hotline phone, which was sitting on her antique nightstand. Only five people knew the number, including two senior staff at State Animal Rescue and two from Faber Animal Shelter. The only other person who knew it was Gabe Cabalo, her married lover.

A chill descended from the whirling overhead fan and crept under her nightie, finding the nerve endings along her spine — or was the chill generated from that annoying chirping sound?

During the fourth bird tune, Mango, her plump, orange tabby was deciding whether to swat it or go back to sleep. Curled up next to the cell phone, she settled on an expression of displeasure and closed her eyes.

The caller was Jessie from H.M.R.U., the Honolulu team in charge of marine mammal rescue throughout Hawai'i. Jolted awake, Rosie clenched the skinny throat of the fuchsia phone and barked, without first clearing the night remnants from her own throat, "What is it?" Her raspy voice cracked, startling both of them. Mango opened her eyes slightly with feigned curiosity.

"Sorry about the wake-up call, but we have a pygmy in trouble at Sugar Beach. It's near the canoe club. A volunteer on an overnight turtle patrol discovered the whale floating near the shore. Her name is Karina Johnsen. She's monitoring the situation and I'm calling agencies. You want her cell number or can you get there right away?"

"I can be there in ten minutes flat," growled Rosie, suddenly alert. She rolled her youthful 44 year-old body off the bed and pulled a tee shirt over her perky, silicone-enhanced chest.

Normally, she dressed her curvy five-foot body with dallied precision, but considering the emergency she decided that denim shorts, a small dark-gray tee shirt, and rubber slippers were enough for public consumption. After ten seconds, she gave up the battle with her long black hair. Fashion could wait.

The veterinarian grabbed her emergency pouch of medicine and equipment and ran from her condo to the elevator. The slow-rising sun, making its way up the backside of Haleakala, would not begin to shed light on Kihei for another 30 minutes.

The moonless night kept the shallow waters off Sugar Beach bathed in darkness, although faint silver specks of light danced on top of the gentle surf like fireflies. Steady, easygoing waves caressed the slight slope of fine sand, bringing ashore the familiar smell of the sea.

A few flashlights from the beach sent narrow streaks of light haphazardly across the sand, but the heaviest cluster of light-beams illuminated the surf that washed over the whale. Rosie headed toward the focus of those beams, unable to recognize any of the shadowy figures in the water.

The serene lapping at the shoreline and the subdued beach chatter were misleading. Thirty feet from the shore a group of nervous rescuers were trying to help the troubled animal. They lacked life-saving skills, and Rosie sensed their anxiety. The eight-foot, pygmy sperm-whale floundered lethargically on the ocean bottom.

"Is Karina here?"

"Yes, over here! Are you the vet?" Although nervous, Karina's body was charged with adrenaline; she was determined to save this whale. Earlier, her soft voice had brought a small degree of calm and order to the group. Her silhouette was striking even in the poor light, towering over the other rescuers.

"Yeah, what's the situation?" Rosie yelled. She plowed through the water and was soon up to her neck in surf.

"We can't guide her out, but otherwise she seems fine," Karina blurted. "I have no idea if her breathing is normal. Sometimes she rolls over. She's *determined* to beach herself!"

Rosie assessed the futile rescue effort without speaking a word. The rescuers stopped their pushing as Rosie stared silently through the early morning.

Finally, she turned her concentration from the whale to Karina, whose soft Scandinavian face and tall stature seemed to belong on a fashion runway.

She noticed that Karina spoke with a tenacious grit, even though her large blue-gray eyes showed unmistakable fear.

"How do you know it's female?" Rosie snapped.

"I don't. Instinct maybe. I feel it! I really don't know."

"Listen up, gang," Rosie ordered, sounding like a drill sergeant. Her bark was more impressive than the faint image of her head, bobbing above the waves, and looking like a short-necked turtle caught in the light chop of the sea.

"You there! Get in front," she ordered, pointing to a young man. "Hold the bottom of the jaw. And *don't* touch this animal anywhere else! This baby is already traumatized from your touching and pushing. Let's make *damn* sure the surf doesn't push us further into the beach. I need another guy to help me back by the tail." The guys quickly took position as the others stepped back.

"Karina, I want you by my side holding my medical pouch. You can sprinkle water over its back, but *please* don't get water in the blowhole. The rest of you... thanks for your help. Return to the beach quietly and tell the flashlight brigade that I need more light on the tail. Let's keep the noise down for just a minute, folks. I want this animal calm, so I can inject the steroids."

Relieved with the change of command, Karina gratefully accepted the entrusted role of assistant. She felt destined to help the pygmy, but there was more. An emotional bond had already formed between her and the whale. Her heart had been racing right alongside the pounding heart of the traumatized pygmy. She knew it was far more than the natural bond between victim and rescuer; she felt a connection of heart and soul.

The size of the gigantic needle that Rosie chose for the injection looked terrifying, and the small group watched in horror. All were silent.

Two volunteers from Karina's overnight turtle patrol watched from the shore, alongside a group of curious onlookers. The beach area started to brighten, bringing hope for the new day. State and local marine agency personnel arrived, along with the Maui police.

"She's going out!" someone yelled from the shore. The beach erupted in cheers, sounding like applause at a rock concert.

"Bless your heart," said Karina softly to herself. The sleek pygmy whale (someone on the beach had already named her "Squirt") headed directly out to sea. With the early dawn illuminating her journey, and the beach gang shouting encouragement, the whale once again appeared strong. The steroid-boost, as well as the careful approach, appeared to be the right medicine for the highly intelligent cetacean.

Rosie yelled, "Go, baby, go!"

"Bless you," Karina called out.

Soon the small sperm whale was nearly out of sight; everyone was still cheering. The guys exchanged high-fives. Flipping her wet black hair backwards, Rosie turned toward the shore and smiled. Even louder applause erupted from the crowd. Karina stood firm in the water, never once taking her attention from Squirt.

"Thanks, everyone, for your help," said Rosie, enjoying the adulation.

Karina suddenly moaned, "Oh, my God!"

"Shit! What the hell..." shouted Rosie, turning to see the whale charging toward her like a blunt-nosed torpedo. With their underslung lower jaws and bullet-like bodies, pygmy whales resemble sharks, and this one was aiming straight at the rescuers. Squirt suddenly slowed down, gliding once again into the shallow waters off Sugar Beach and directly into the outstretched arms of Karina. Then the pygmy coughed.

"I need permission for a truck and a sling as soon as possible," Rosie yelled to the woman on the shoreline from the DNLR. She stroked Squirt's nose and spoke softly. "What's wrong with you, baby?" Karina was crying softly and the guys were waiting for orders.

"This baby has some kind of lung problem," Rosie said. "I'll administer an antibiotic, but then all we can do is to wait for the portable tank. It's something internal. Obviously, she has some crazy instinct to return to the beach and... to us."

"Just tell me what I can do," said Karina between muffled sobs.

"Stay right here," Rosie answered. "She seems to favor you."

It took four hours to get the whale hoisted out of the water and transported to the large holding tank at the Ocean Center. Squirt's breathing became labored by the time Rosie could do a superficial examination inside the tank and determine her sex. The cuts and scrapes across the prune-like skin appeared to be normal, most likely from coral.

"Acute pneumonia," said Rosie. "Rapid irregular breathing, coughing, sneezing. They get all the *stuff* that humans get. I've given this girl everything I can for the time being. Another hour will tell."

Circling the outer wall of the tank, Squirt was

clearly struggling to breathe. Thirty minutes later, it was apparent that she was gasping for breath and barely able to swim.

"I'm sorry, Karina. There's no hope. She's suffering. I have to euthanize her."

"No! No!"

Squirt slowly drifted over to their side of the tank. It wasn't clear that she could make it. With a half-gasp from her blowhole, she came alongside the tank wall, turned ever so slightly on her side and rubbed against Karina's outstretched arm.

"I'm so sorry," stuttered Rosie, tears flowing down her cheeks, as her long needle found its mark next to the heart. Squirt looked up — deep into Karina's eyes — and took her last breath.

TRIBAL ECLECTIC

"That was my ex-girlfriend you spent the morning with!" Sky exclaimed with alarm.

Two days after her whale-rescue ordeal, Karina Johnsen was sitting on a large, leopard-print floor pillow at the luxurious Wailea home of her boyfriend, professional artist Sky Shafer.

"Tribal eclectic" was the term Sky often used to describe the interior of his home. The collection of tribal art, along with small herds of carved elephants, giraffes, and zebras turned the living room into a wild and earthy African experience. Charismatic Balinese bird sculptures, strung from the lanai ceiling, glided back and forth in the breeze. The other rooms were arbitrarily stylized and hopelessly mismatched, a pad that brought grins of approval from his bachelor friends.

As soon as Sky heard Karina's story, he knew the vet was his former girlfriend, Rosie Faber. Nervously, he listened. Finally, he started to relax when it became apparent that Rosie was unaware of his relationship with Karina. But he had good reason to worry.

"She was totally professional," said Karina. "I never thought to ask her name."

"You must be emotionally drained from it."

"It's hard to think about that little whale... I felt such a connection; it was like losing a sister. But, I had no idea Rosie was your ex-girlfriend."

"It's weird all right," said Sky, feeling uncomfortable with the idea of Karina being anywhere near Rosie. "She's an expert with animals, maybe the best marine specialist on the island. At least that sick animal had good care."

One of Karina's long legs, lightly sprinkled with freckles, was stretched out; the other one was crossed under her rump, positioned like a slim, sinuous cheetah resting on a small knoll. The white plumeria flower displayed over her left ear softened her flaming red hair, and a colorful dress accentuated her creamy Norwegian-born complexion.

"Why can't you find some wall space for your wonderful seascapes?" asked Karina. "I'm not suggesting you move your Zulu masks, or anything like that — but it would be nice to see a few Shafers here."

"I kind of like the aura of other cultures around here. It's my antidote for rock fever. And besides, I'm not sure my herds could compete with a bunch of reef fish."

Sky and Karina had been in a fun-filled relationship since meeting a couple of months ago on the top of Haleakala, the island's 10,000-foot volcano. They joked that their relationship could only go down hill from there. Seven years younger, Karina would soon join him in the forty-something club. In heels, the six-foot former model stood eyeball-to-eyeball with him.

Their relationship was in the "early-glow" stage; it held the excitement of dating topped off with the security of a monogamous relationship. The idea of living together hadn't popped up — neither one was ready to make a full-blown commitment.

Sky sat on the floor, his square jaw peering over his knees. His forehead hinted at a rigorous life, and the scars hidden under his thick, sandy-blond hair confirmed it. They looked like the racetrack after a demolition derby.

"It's a shame I didn't know who that little black-haired tart was, or I could have spent the morning picking her brain on the idiosyncrasies of Mr. Safari Shafer."

Sky visibly twitched. "See, I have an angel watching over me. Now is my red-headed cheetah ready to lap up another glass of wine?"

"OK, but when you return there's something I should mention," she said pensively.

"Be right back." To lighten the mood he rolled on his back and then sprang up like a gymnast. The agile move seemed effortless. He was in good shape from paddling with the Makena outrigger-canoe team, hiking in the mountains, performing Tantric workouts, and occasionally chasing a felon through a lava tube. He quickly returned with two glasses of wine filled to the rim and joined her on the pillow.

"Thanks, sweetie," she said, taking a sip. "I hate saying this, but there's something you should know."

"What's that?"

"There's a rumor about you that's been floating around."

"Really, what rumor?"

"Well, it was told to me like this: 'Sky had an affair with a local Portuguese woman during his relationship with Rosie, and apparently that was the last straw for her.'"

25

Sky chuckled. "That's a good one. And I'd sure love to know what the earlier straws were."

"I first heard it a month ago," admitted Karina, "and thought it was a joke. I wasn't going to mention it, but recently I heard it again."

"It's ridiculous and it's also a little sick. Why in the hell a *Portuguese* woman? Anyway, who cares? I can't do anything about it."

For him, guessing the source of the innuendo was as clear as the sparkling turquoise waters off his lanai. The timing was a surprise, since he had broken up with Rosie over a year ago, and they had lived together only a few months. He knew their relationship didn't end well, but why start a rumor now? It seemed like a long time ago.

Rumors on Maui gusted as frequently and briskly as the afternoon trade winds. The trades, whipped up in the hot sugar cane fields of the central valley, typically swirled through North Kihei. Then the fickle air mingled with the sea breezes and blew into South Kihei and Wailea. Cane dust and toxic rumor were as much a part of this paradise island as the swaying of coconut palms.

"I confess to having my share of relationships over the years, but most of those flings eventually turned into lasting friendships." And then he thought about a couple of exceptions — memories that had shaken his trust in women.

"However, there's one thing you need to know about me." He paused for effect. "I'm a confirmed serial monogamist."

"Really, I believe you. Besides, my lead detective hasn't dug up anything in his sexual activities report. He did say that his team hasn't even scratched the surface of your earlier years."

"Yeah, yeah, real funny," he said with a half smile. How ironic, he thought, that it was so far from the truth. More than once he had to defend himself from being sexually assaulted in prison during some of those early years.

"Is it true that all three of Rosie's ex-husbands are dead?" Karina asked abruptly, her eyes growing larger.

"Scary, huh?" he replied, looking concerned again. "None of them made it to their 45th birthday. One had a heart attack and the other two were freaky accidents. I always wondered if there was some kind of curse. It was a little spooky for me to break off that relationship with her."

"Lucky you two didn't marry. Maybe the curse was being married to her. How come he had a heart attack at that young age?"

"Well... I'm a little uncomfortable saying this. I haven't told anyone. I hate talking about other people, not to mention someone who's dead."

"You know I won't say anything."

Sky took a few deep breaths before he continued. "Once, after far too many wines, she confessed to me that her first husband died on top of her. Apparently he had a weak heart. He died from exhaustion trying to satisfy her demanding sexual appetite. She pushed him off and rolled him to the side of the bed. Maybe it wasn't entirely her fault, but her excesses had pushed him too far. I mean he wasn't the strongest guy around. I suppose you could say that in a way she killed him. At least she was partially responsible... like an accessory to it."

His tone became even more serious. "Right after she told me, I arranged for a complete heart checkup. Luckily, she never remembered talking about it. So, what do you think?"

"I think it's sad. Such a young man. I would need to know more of their history to make a judgment. Bless them both. I feel sorry for them. Actually, I know a woman that lost her husband that way. It's not unusual. And it's been great fodder for jokes over the years. Who hasn't kidded about it?"

"Ha, ha — I know, I've joked about it too. Sometimes the heart can take a pounding. I only told you because you won't pass it along, and besides we're joined at the hip."

Karina softened her eyes and looked directly at Sky. "Joined at the hip, huh. Nice thought. You know I love being here and being part of your animal kingdom."

"Well, I'm lucky I found you, kitten. Right now you look like a helpless jungle cat waiting for the king of beasts." He lifted his eyebrows with unmistakable clarity. "I should get my camera to capture that pose."

"Bring your zoom lens, big boy, and I'll extend it to telephoto," she purred. "I guarantee you'll bag your limit so don't get carried away and exceed your, um... quota."

"Not a chance, but I'll need to untangle those long legs first."

VOLCANIC VIXENS

On that same evening, the Vixens had a dinner scheduled for Tommy Bahama's Restaurant. Rosie Faber was primping for it in her Ma'alaea condo. Jokingly calling themselves the "Volcanic Vixens," Rosie's gang enjoyed a special camaraderie when the subject turned to men, which it often did.

Rosie had gone through four significant relationships, including three marriages, by her 43rd birthday. The marriages seemed happy and she had spoken well of her husbands. Later, after every divorce, she admitted the difficulties — how each husband had abused her in some fashion.

"Damn these wobbly pieces of crap," Rosie mumbled. "Just to attract some dumb bastard who might buy me a drink..." She was struggling to get her high-arched feet through the triple maze of straps attached to her shiny black, four-inch heels.

Mango watched in amusement and, at the same time, tracked the approach of a small lizard, foolishly climbing down the bedroom wall in a series of tantalizing quick darts. The orange tabby figured that the scrawny pupu would be more palatable after an hour of chase and torment.

With the polished stilts secured, Rosie wobbled

out of the condo. Her jet-black Mazda Miata waited five flights below. She didn't notice Mango's eyes getting larger.

She drove over to Gecko Kaneshiro's cottage, which was stuffed into one of the car-cluttered neighborhoods in North Kihei. It was a small one-bedroom near the beach with an outrageous monthly rent. The driveway was full, so she parked between two cars on the street. She squeezed in close, knowing it was unlikely the battered Maui cruisers were going anywhere soon, since the hoods were up and the engines were gone.

"Chardonnay?" asked Gecko (all her friends called her Gecko rather than her real name, Kako). This, before Rosie got past the screen door.

The clutter in the living room mirrored the untidy ambience of the neighborhood. Gecko pushed a few bottles of oils to the end of the massage table and plopped down two "hang loose" coasters for the glasses. The wine bar was open.

"Sure, I need to mellow. I was thinking about Sky on the way over. Those months were some of the most turbulent of my life."

"Wasn't that a couple years ago?"

"Fourteen months, but it's like yesterday," she snapped.

"Maybe you're still healing."

Gecko knew her friend needed to talk and it would take more than one glass of wine before she finished. Once Rosie started to gossip, her marathon motor mouth would ease into the fast lane of the speedway and take a few laps. When she ran out of gas and took a pit stop, her friends would jump in and made a quick change of subject.

The Vixens loved her anyway, and enjoyed the

prolonged rounds of gossip. Doing the Daytona with Rosie meant being privy to some of the island's juiciest morsels of chat. Today she took Gecko by surprise and pulled into the pit after one quick lap.

"What's new with you?"

"Um... I had the yummiest guy in today for a massage. Maybe a little young but he loved my touch. He groaned like he was about to... well, you know."

Thirty-six years of weathering had not penetrated Gecko's young Japanese face; her baby fat appeared permanent. Playful, sexy, and slightly shy of five feet, she constantly bubbled with excitement.

It had been over a decade since Gecko had a serious relationship. Her buddies guessed it was because of her horselaugh, which gathered a deeper staccato bellow after a few margaritas.

"It must be tough massaging those muscle-bound surfer knots. And another thing, with your strong hands it must be hard on them." Rosie winked. She loved teasing her libidinous pal. "Too bad they're all so young," she added with a mock look of concern.

"Yeah. Now it's the kiteboarders moving in. Those kids are strange, even for me. They're flying in the air doing their flips and twists."

Off the coasts of Maui, kiteboarders practice aerial acrobatics and flight simulation. On most days, the winds are favorable on one side of the island or the other. After completing their sky maneuvers, they land upright on their strapped-on boards and surf away for another flight. Often they wipe out as they crash into the choppy sea. Solo sailors on Ma'alaea Bay have a choice of being wind-propelled across the waves at 60 miles-per-hour by a colorful sail, or being wind-yanked through the air at exhilarating speeds

31

by an erratic kite. The inevitable entanglements occasionally lead to territorial conflict.

"I'm ready to party," announced Rosie.

After they rinsed their glasses, they grabbed their evening gear and headed outside into the night.

"Maybe I should have left the top up. Our hair might take a beating, but it gives the guys something to stare at along the way."

"You should have a big, shiny, Cadillac convertible. Nobody will see us in this little thing."

"Yeah, right. Is everyone showing up tonight?"

"Just us and Liz. The others have dates."

They headed for the Wailea restaurant via the beach route. At the intersection of South Kihei Road they waited to turn. Rosie searched for a gap through the two long lines of cars.

"Shit, you've got to dart out halfway and straddle the center stripe," said Rosie. "And hope to hell both lanes slam on their brakes at the same time."

"At least they're considerate around here," said Gecko. "I haven't heard the sound of a horn in years. Besides, everybody knows that Kihei stands for 'No Left Turn.'"

Rosie saw a small gap and accelerated into the northbound lane. Halfway across the street, she looked down the southbound lane and panicked. A tractor-trailer rig was heading her way. A crash played across her imagination. The images seemed so real, so vivid, and so frightening that her eyes closed tighter and tighter.

As her car stalled, she watched the monster semi truck zigzag across the center line. She feared the out-of-control rig would jackknife. The massive truck tires grew larger with every rotation, dwarfing her midget Miata. Howling masses of hot rubber bumped along the pavement; the truck bed lurched louder and louder. The smell of axle grease began to fill her nostrils.

Outwardly, Rosie was stalled in a state of paralysis while, inside her sub-conscious, panic and doom raged on. She heard the warning blasts of an air horn, the screeching of brakes.

Rows of tires charged toward her. They were thumping and coming closer. Strangely, long tree branches jutted from every one of the wheel wells and stretched across the center stripe, far into her lane. In her mind she could smell the fresh cut, forest-scented wood. The branches, stripped of their bark, seemed shaped to the razor sharpness of a samurai sword, waiting to slice off her head. The chilling thought of cold steel made her shudder.

Reaching across the street and carving up the air, fine-honed blades were only one of her worries. Under frozen eyelids, her eyes twitched repeatedly from images of the tall, top-heavy semi trailer flipping over and burying her car with its load. She strained to see the contents. Maybe it was empty. The trailer leaned over, precariously teetering on one set of tires. Everything was suddenly quiet. She fought to see inside. She had always dreaded suffocating. Something snapped. Her eyes opened. The big rig had crawled to a stop.

"Jesus, Rosie, what's the matter? Go ahead, everyone's waiting for us."

They both looked at the two lanes of stalled vehicles, drivers patiently waiting with their horns untouched. As Rosie drove into the empty lane, the truck driver stuck his hand out the window and flashed the friendly shaka sign. Mature palm trees, bundled for transplant to a new Wailea home site, extended past the rear of the tailgate.

"What's wrong? You OK?"

"Yeah, yeah! I'm OK! I thought that big rig would... never mind."

Rosie and Gecko rode the covered outdoor escalator to the second floor. Gecko led the way into Tommy Bahama's, making a colorful, showy entry. Rosie, on the other hand, was dressed entirely in black, matching her hair. If Tommys' had a black-walled foyer, she would have entered unseen.

While Tommy's occasionally served up opportunities for the gossip gang to physically connect with the opposite sex, the arty bamboo-laden lounge routinely served as the epicenter for firing accusations toward bygone men.

Past flames and ex-husbands were symbolically roasted there on a smoldering table of lava, while being served searing doses of Vixen venom. Exaggerated tales of past love, future sex, and present male contempt dominated barroom conversation. They shared their stories over slurps of margaritas, strawberry daiquiris, and the powerful, "man-slamming" triple-rum tonic Bahama Mama.

As soon as the two Vixens settled into a favorite table, someone from the bar shouted, "Rosie!" Startled, Rosie nearly jumped out of her seat. Then she turned and recognized the bartender.

"Hey, Peter! Howzit?"

"Good to see you guys. Your server's on the way."

"You have such a great memory for names," Gecko said to Rosie. "You're always remembering someone's birthday or their latest problem. You must know half the people on the island. Why so jumpy today?"

"It's *nothing*. Just the traffic. Tell me, you think Sky is still seeing that Portuguese woman from Makawao? Lately, my church group's been obsessed with the subject of infidelity."

"I heard from one of the gals at the Cultural Center that he was seeing someone called Karina. She's the one who opened that little nightclub called 'Local Styling' in Kihei. It's at the ass end of Kukui Mall. Local musicians play jazz and blues."

"Karina? That's interesting. I just met someone named Karina at Sugar Beach. I wonder... Is she tall and slim? Red hair?"

"No idea."

"This woman helped me on that whale rescue. She formed some kind of bond with the whale. But she was far too sweet for the likes of Sky Shafer."

"I bet he's still seeing that Portuguese chick on the side," said Gecko. "Men! They're all dickheads!"

Gecko perpetuated gossip. It seemed likely to her that a good-looking man like Sky would have an affair. After all, having a fling on a hot sensuous island was as popular as taking a warm dip in the beckoning beach waters.

"Hell with him! I wish he would take a *permanent* trip off island. Enough about him already, did you hear the report on the reason those three whales died?"

"No."

"It was all about noise affecting the whales in these shallow waters when that *damn* navy conducts their underwater LFA sound experiments. The tests were the reason those three humpbacks washed ashore. Shattered eardrums! The necropsies found nothing else wrong with them. Hell, it's criminal. Bad enough they have to deal with mercury poisoning, drift nets, and ship collisions."

"Jesus, Rosie, you sure get personal with your animals. That front page picture in the Maui News of you and the pygmy whale was heartbreaking."

"It's my job, poor helpless creatures. But it was painful to watch her sad face right before I had to euthanize her."

"Did you say necropsy?" asked Gecko suddenly. "Spare me the dissecting details while I'm eating this spring roll. Too bad you weren't better at dissecting the problems with all those men you married. Maybe they were poor picks, but they still didn't deserve their fate, especially number three — Roger the Rat, as you called him."

Rosie sneered, "Did you say picks or pricks?"

Before they moved over to a dinner table, Liz called and begged off the dinner. Rosie had tried to keep the conversation from being too funny, since Gecko's abrasive volume had risen with each Bahama Mama, and a number of other patrons had glanced their way. The braying laughter had even turned heads along the bamboo-lined corners of the far wall.

Annoyed with the noise, and still reeling from the memory of the tractor-trailer rig, Rosie faked one of her legendary migraines and called off the rest of the evening. Then she thought, once again, about Sky.

HANA HOU

Outside his three-car garage in Wailea, Sky lowered the top and warmed up his ivory 1973 5.3 "E" Jaguar convertible. The deep-throated classic was perfect for cornering the narrow road to Hana. The oval chrome grille was well designed for splattering the plethora of jungle bugs along the way.

Karina looked forward to the festive getaway weekend. It was going to be her first experience at the East Maui Taro Festival, held annually in April. She tied down her straw sun hat and curled her legs into the soft-leather bucket seat.

"Hang on to your hat," said Sky, "and try not to swallow too many bugs. It should be a gorgeous ride. The waterfalls will be roaring after all the rain lately." He worried they might run into Rosie this weekend, and dreaded a confrontation. Since the breakup, he had only seen her from a distance; but even from afar he could feel her penetrating "stink eye."

"Just keep it under a hundred on the hairpin turns, Andretti."

As the crow flies, or more likely, as the high-flying Hawaiian petrel soars, the coastal town of Hana was east of Wailea. But the majestic Haleakala capably filled the space between. It made passage into the remote area of Hana a formidable challenge as the 50 miles of narrow, curvy turns often hugged the cliff's edge.

Most visitors drove leisurely, making frequent and risky pit stops. They favored taking photos on crumbling, century-old bridges, on the back edges of fragile landslide turnouts, and in streams prone to flash floods. Sounds of "take one more step back, honey" and "it's probably not deep" pierced the balmy, aromatic air along the road to Hana.

Driving past Paia and the world-famous windsurfing mecca of Hookipa, the cloudless skies held; it looked like a perfect day for the exciting ride.

Soon they reached the rugged jungle road with its "toot the horn" turns and scenic cliffs. Whiffs of perfumed plants flooded the open two-seater every time Sky downshifted for one of the 600-odd curves. They pulled over to explore a popular waterfall.

"Wait while I pick up a few of these guavas," said Karina. "Their fragrance is driving me crazy."

"Take your time. It's fun playing tourist. When you're ready, let's walk up to the pool. We can take a quick dip if you like."

Before reaching the falls, they took time to suck on a few guavas, debating the techniques of spitting or swallowing the seeds. Karina thought spitting them to propagate the species was the natural thing to do, while the guava guru felt that ingesting the crunchy nuggets garnished their true flavor.

They watched the flurry of water spill over white polished rocks and into a tranquil pool. Flaming-orange Chinese tulips were floating in a symmetrical arrangement over the silver-gray pool. Sunrays blazed through the forest clearing, igniting the brilliant orange flowers, and speckling the circular surface with a garden of bright, fanciful bulbs. The pond was still, except for the cascading sheen of cool mountain water tumbling down the back wall.

It was a setting reminiscent of canvas — not something captured on film — and not one of the tourists standing at the water's edge dared enter and disturb the natural perfection.

When they returned to the Jag, rental cars had filled every conceivable parking spot, and the tourists were piling out with their cameras.

"Hop in before we get tourist-trapped," said Sky, laughing.

Back on the slender road, the low-slung curvy roadster, with its flared wheel arches and deep-bass rumble, attracted plenty of notice from the oncoming cars. Sky roared across the historic one-lane bridges, slowing down every time he saw a rainbow eucalyptus, his favorite roadside tree. The painter admired how the brilliant orange stripes streaking down the fat trunks invited the eye to the delicate brushstrokes of lime green, leaving the muted mauve, rust, tan, and gray colors unnoticed. Despite the scenic lulls, they made it to Hana in "Jag time."

For the past ten years Sky had made a reservation at his favorite cottage one full year in advance. It was a funky place all right: scantily furnished, pleading for paint, and loaded with mismatched silverware that had tasted the tongues of thousands. But it was only a short walk to the Hana ballpark, home of the annual taro event.

The check-in procedure was always the same. Mrs. Namuro, the diminutive proprietor, was slouched in her large overstuffed chair. A hand-painted "Cash-Only" sign was displayed on her well worn desk. In spite of her advancing age, her vacation rental business was quite orderly.

"OK, I'll make a reservation for next year; but you should know that I'll probably not be around," she said in her sweet, soft voice.

"I hope you'll be here, Mrs. Namuro. Hana wouldn't be the same without you," said Sky in a mimicking sweet tone. He gave her a sexy wink and she blushed. He was never sure if her threatened exodus was for physical, emotional, or financial reasons. Whatever the implication, she was always waiting for him with a conspiratorial smile.

"I'll get the bags," Sky told Karina as they walked to the cottage. "You can open her up."

"OK, but I have to pick some of these plumerias on the way."

The best feature of the cottage, other than the in-town location, was the second story view deck overlooking the steep street that flowed down to the harbor. In the distance, the Hana Hotel chip-and-putt course was laid out on a lush hillside. The view included stately junipers framing the rain-nourished fairways.

The entire deck décor consisted of a small wood table that hadn't felt the hairs of a paintbrush in many years, and two wobbly red-cushioned chairs. They were collected by Mrs. Namuro from a Kahului garage sale 15 years ago for the sum of two dollars, and had been heavily tax-depreciated ever since.

Sky returned annually to Paradise Cottage so he could sit on the deck and watch the characters of Hana drive up and down the street. Conveniently, the corrugated tin roof hung far enough over the narrow deck for guests to "talk story," even during a downpour.

During the last decade, the only things that

changed in the cottage were 60 watt light bulbs and his companion. Karina was his fourth significant other. He was hopeful she would be the final one, but he had also been hopeful about the other three.

"Sweetie, I love this place!"

"Cozy, huh? Before we get settled in, let's stretch our legs and walk to the harbor," suggested Sky.

"Good idea. I guess we don't have to worry about prowlers tonight with this squeaky floor."

"And I brought my boom box to distract any eavesdropping neighbors outside these flimsy walls. That's for later tonight, if you get my drift."

"Sounds like we're covered. Just in case there's any lingering female presence hanging around, I'll cast a small spell... OK, that's done. Let's go."

It took less than an hour to check out the harbor activities and return to the cottage.

"I'll pour the wine," volunteered Karina. "Hope my photos of the Makaliʻi sailing into the harbor turn out. I guess that voyaging canoe has seen plenty of sunsets all over the Pacific. The guys looked hung over. Even the wahine crew looked a bit roughed up, considering they only had to sail from the Big Island."

"Those gals could handle the canoe by themselves. Every one of them can read the night sky better than we can read a Kihei road map. Well, maybe that's not a fair contest. Even locals get confused with all those Hawaiian names."

Karina raised her glass, "Cheers, sweetie!"

"Hipahipa! Here's to a great poi party this weekend," he responded, referring to the gray pasty staple that was a mainstay of the traditional Hawaiian diet.

"That's the *second* time those two couples

drove by in their rented jeep," Sky noted. "She's still reading the map! Two streets in Hana and they're lost. You would think the sight of the ocean might give them a clue as to which way to turn."

Sky had been watching the mix of people drive past, and had settled into the laid-back pace of the isolated community. The flow of wine expanded his humor.

"You'd think so," Karina replied. "Hopefully, she didn't have that map in front of her on the entire trip. So many tourists get back to their condos and wonder what in the world there was to do in Hana. And wonder what the big attraction is. Maybe it's a case of can't see the rainforest for the trees."

"Honey, there they go again! *Third* time! Next time they drive by let's yell out 'turn right.'"

Karina laughed. "Bless their hearts."

From the vantage point of the upper deck, Sky had been making a casual survey of the local trucks passing by.

"Have you noticed how the locals hang their arms out of their trucks?" Sky asked. "Straight down. Limp, hanging onto nothing. It's because the arm catches maximum breeze. I know because I've tried it. Amazing how it cools you off. It's air conditioning local style. You gotta love it here.

"Something else. The town must have a law against driving around in a pickup without an ice chest or a dog in back. Haven't seen an empty truck bed yet. Maybe we should retire here. We've got the huge cooler. Just need a dog."

Before dark they walked once again to Hana Bay. They saw the sleek, highly polished, 40-foot racing outrigger, Kapueokahi, cut across the middle of the bay. Six paddlers from the Hana Canoe Club were training for an upcoming distance regatta off Moloka'i. The black-hulled koa canoe was barely visible on the graying sea, but the quick synchronized strokes of the team flashed against the fading sky. The husky timing chants of the second paddler could be heard across the idyllic inlet.

"They're taking their practice runs seriously this year," admired Sky.

"Sweetie, those grunts are giving me ideas," whispered Karina.

"We could practice our own rhythm chants tonight," he suggested with a familiar twinkle. He found her sensuous allure all the more enchanting in the gentle light.

Their chilled Riesling went especially well with the sunset activities of the local community. Around the old concrete park table, families came and went, drawn to the evening ocean breezes and island-famous Tutu's, a shave-ice snack shop. The Hana area enjoyed the largest settlement of pure Hawaiians in the state and everyone in the park knew each other. It was a remote throwback community where time lingered.

They watched as the canoe team hauled their outrigger onto the black sand beach. Over the last few years, Sky had met most of the other Maui team racers. He was the paddler and bailer in the fourth position of the Makena Canoe Club.

He introduced Karina to the Hana paddlers after the team wiped down their canoe and rig. She loved their ethnic diversity. Like other competition clubs on Maui, the team chose paddlers on merit.

She noticed that both haole women were slender and feminine, and that the short sexy blond had the experience and respect to be the team's steerer.

"Quite a crew," said Karina after they left. "Two haole and two Hawaiian gals, along with a Filipino and a Japanese man."

"It's the melting pot spirit that makes the island special," he added.

They walked out to the end of the old pier, which was still embedded with rusty cattle-train railings from many years past.

"I would have loved to watch the cattle walk the plank to the cargo boats from this little pier," said Karina.

"Actually, the paniolos roped the cows and dragged them into the water where they got harnessed and lifted by a steamer's crane. Giant cranes cranked up the cows by their thick necks. Their stretched-out necks and bodies would swing back and forth from the wind until they were lowered on deck."

"Yuck! That's probably when the humane society first cranked up their own operation," she responded, appalled by the image.

"Most of the Maui cattle were pulled into the ocean at Makena for shipping near Clint Eastwood's new home. Can you picture him sitting on a horse and staring at charging waves while lugging an ornery steer?"

"No."

"Some of the cows became shark food. Did you know our cowboys were the first ones in the country? The Wild West started here. In fact—"

"Honu! Honu!" shouted three adolescent boys, waving enthusiastically for them to come over.

"It's a sea turtle," Karina said, remembering

the Hawaiian word from her volunteer work at the Ocean Center. "Come on!" She grabbed his hand and led him to the edge of the old concrete pier. A prehistoric leathery face rose from the sea, looked toward them, and drew in a breath of air. His oval shell, nearly two feet across, was camouflaged by blends of black and brown countershading.

"There it is — ooh! And another one! And much bigger!" Karina was as excited as the kids. "Look at those haunting black eyes. You know the Hawaiians consider them good luck and symbols of long life. Some families consider them personal protectors. Of all the endangered species, our green sea turtles seem to be making one of the better recoveries, at least around our island."

"Hope some of the boys from Kahului don't find out about their comeback, or we could see 'Tortuga Verde Soup' on the mixed-plate lunch menu," kidded Sky.

Holding hands, they felt especially connected with their environment. The boys were still laughing, but losing interest as the turtles moved away. They expressed their appreciation to the boys for sharing the discovery.

Sky said, "I must get back here and do another painting with a few ghost crabs in the foreground, the old pier in the middle, and in the distance that knobby island catching the end of a screaming red sunset. Maybe with a pair of large bobbing turtles sticking their necks out and sucking air in front of that banged-up wharf."

"More of your harmony in nature, huh?"

"Hana, hana hou," he joked (Hana, let's do it again).

"Let's have another encore performance tomorrow night on Hana Bay. Oh, and don't forget we have another bottle of wine."

"I accept. But now you're making me stagger up that steep hill to get to our little nest," she said with a playful groan.

"I'll make it up to you when we get there. I'm going to ravish you until you beg for mercy. Plan on hours of tingles and throbs."

"Hmmm. Will I need to do anything other than switch positions for your animal savagery?" purred Karina, completely ignoring the steep incline.

"I was hoping you would make coffee in the morning."

As soon as they returned, Sky tuned in a jazz station on the boom box and went to the greasy kitchen drawer for a corkscrew. He had to yank at it a couple of times, as the warped wooden artifact was permanently askew. Karina was already unbuttoning her blouse.

"Sweetie, I'm taking this grimy body into the shower."

"I love it when you talk dirty," he bantered.

"Be a darling and bring me a glass of wine. I'll need some grape hydration for the primping stage. I'm already wet from your proposal, so don't get lost, big boy."

"Don't worry. I plan to limber up my muscles while you're in the bathroom. No, not *that* muscle. That's your part."

"Hmmm, I'll gloss my lips."

Sky occasionally engaged in preliminary stretches before his love bouts with Karina. His unique approach of replacing toning workouts with lovemaking came after some pleasant experimentation.

He discovered that he built up better endurance this way than from his former workouts on the Stairmaster. Pull-ups, pushups, and assorted creative thrusts gave him better toning than all the chin-bars, barbells, and Bowflex Motivators at the gym.

At the musty gym he was generally bored within an hour, but his hard Tantric approach allowed him unlimited hours of enjoyment. His technique was far more than a toning workout; he loved bringing pleasure to Karina, and he couldn't imagine making love without being in love.

Karina loved the marathon love romps, and recognized the health benefits of her own active participation. She loved frolicking for as long as Sky could last.

In what seemed like an eternity to Sky, but in reality was only 20 minutes, Karina emerged from the bathroom with a sultry smile that suggested good things to come.

"I'm ready for your up and coming extravaganza, sailor. Everything in the bedroom is oooooh so perfect. Nice touches: jazz music, sealed windows, gentle breeze from the ceiling fan, and red plumeria petals across the bed. You must have taken Romance 101 in college."

"Not really, but I did read, *The Idiots' Guide to Wooing Your Woman.* Let's start with you dropping that robe and spreading that Norwegian flesh across the bed."

"Oooooh-oooooh," she hummed.

"There's an erogenous zone here." He nibbled between her peach-colored toes.

"Really," she sighed, her voice sinking to a fuzzy whisper.

Sky took a couple of back roads along the journey, and occasionally paused for small sips of wine. Karina also reached for her wine glass and silently gave a toast to her lover. Expertly, she swirled her tongue around the fermented liquid as a warm wave of anticipation rose to a crescendo.

Karina let out a scream, celebrating her first crest of the night. Wave upon warm wave crested and overflowed.

Sky looked up, caught his breath, and smiled. "Care to get in a few licks?"

"Your wish, master, is my pleasure," she panted. "This might take awhile." She nibbled on his ears playfully and then tenderly worked her way down.

They fondled and cuddled while time disappeared, then tumbled into deep sleep.

TAROFEST

A driving Hana rain provided a convenient sound cover for Sky and Karina's lovemaking encore the next morning, replacing Hawaiian harmonies from the boom-box. The pounding on the metal roof and the pounding against the firm mattress finally gave way to doves cooing and pink sunrays splashing across the bedroom. Karina's long Scandinavian body glistened on top of the white cotton sheet like the sprinkling of morning dew.

It was time to hoof it over to the park to join paniolos, kupuna, hula dancers, hippies, musicians, taro farmers, canoe carvers, spiritual healers, poi makers, vendors, "locals," tourists, and other eclectic Maui folks at the annual springtime East Maui Taro Festival.

"It's a pretty big park for a little community," said Karina, walking up the narrow street. "Those giant tents cover half the ballpark."

"Yeah, lots of stuff in there."

"I can't wait to check out all the craft booths. Look! They're building a racing canoe under that long tent."

"Looks like they got to third base with it," kidded Sky, noting the near-completed outrigger stretched over huge wooden cradles at the edge of the infield diamond. "I read that it took 50 guys in relay teams to carry that koa log from the forest. It's amazing they even found koa on this island. Most of it was cut years ago.

"Listen, honey, first thing we tackle is the taro seafood chowder," announced the ten-year veteran. "The creamy stuff is to die for, but they usually run out early. It comes in a big Styrofoam container with huge chunks of ono fish; even the lumpy taro is heavenly. That should tide us over while we check out the arts and crafts."

"Yum."

"Later we can dive into the kim-chee tako poke and some guri-guri with taro. If you're still standing we can polish off some taro-kulolo ice cream."

"Listen, chowderhead. How about I just get a taro smoothie and curl up in front of the band?" suggested Karina, grinning.

High above, a flock of great frigatebirds was circling the festival. The black predators soared in the pale sky as they waited for startled, low-flying boobies to cater their seafood breakfast. Scissor-shaped, seven-foot wingspans assured delivery.

"I wonder if those frigatebirds can smell the chowder?" asked Sky.

"Hope not, this tent's too small for those thieves."

An hour after savoring the rich lumpy chowder they compromised by splitting a "Big Boy Plate." It was well known on the island that the largest-bodied vendors sold the biggest and best plate lunches. Spotting the largest cook was quicker than inspecting the ingredients in each of the dozen food stalls. They carted off the takeout box, stuffed with chow mein, shrimp fu yung, and taro/ulu tempura.

"Too bad the special didn't include a porter to lug this to the lunch tent," said Karina. She moved toward one of the picnic tables. "Let's squeeze in over there."

Under the large canvas mess tent, tables were jammed with festival revelers talking, laughing, whistling, and gobbling up the jumbo food containers.

During their feasting, she leaned over to Sky and whispered, "Look around. If Maui is the friendliest place in the country, the people in Hana have to get the trophy for biggest hearts. Everyone's joking around and swapping their food. It's really a special community."

"There's only one."

"I want to become an annual groupie. Can we 'Hana hou' next year?"

"Absolutely, assuming Mrs. Namuro holds our reservation." Like the tentative property manager, he thought of his relationships — week by week. Long-range trust and commitment had been elusive for him since prison, and would take time.

From their table, they watched the hula dancers, aged 4 to 84, spread out across the expansive grassy area. Hula groups were represented from each part of Maui. The keiki were the biggest crowd pleasers, and the barefoot four-year-old darlings were stealing the show by mimicking the undulating motion of their elders with their tiny hands and hips.

After watching the groups perform, they spotted a poi-making demonstration. The taro root had already been cooked, and now the purple paste was being mashed inside a hollowed-out stone. They watched as it was pounded and mashed into a "one-finger" consistency. They learned that the thicker the poi, the fewer fingers needed to scoop it up.

Sky said, "Let's split up for an hour. Give you some quality time for rummaging through the craft booths, and I can give the volunteers a break at the Food Bank booth. I have an affiliation with them, and this will give me a chance to help out a little. After you find the perfect gift for that special person in your life, wander over to the humanities tent. I'll introduce you to our food distribution gang."

"You're a volunteer, huh? Quite commendable. I like your shopping idea, though. I'll hunt down some jewelry for that special person, and according to my 'More Self, More Power' class — that would be me. See you."

Karina wandered over to the band and approached them as they were leaving the stage.

"Howzit? I loved that last jazzy number," she said with a smile. "How about putting together some Hawaiian songs with a little bluesy beat for my nightclub in Kihei? Here's my card."

"So you da cheeck," said the ukulele player. "Heard 'bout dat club. Next month we bring you one bluesy show. Now we late already for odda gig. OK, we call ya mo' later?"

"Sure. Love your music. Look forward to hearing you play again. Aloha."

"Aloha. See ya."

Karina walked over to the first booth. Large, colorful quilts hung on the tent walls; smaller ones were stacked on tables. Many of the vibrant designs featured a particular flower. The rich colors of white ginger, anthurium, maile, poinsettia, and silversword dazzled the eye. Karina learned that each quilt had more than a million stitches, and took over a thousand hours of work to complete.

She lingered before the regal pattern of the Hawaiian flag, and then stood in awe before a large quilt featuring the crown of Queen Lili'uokalani, proudly crafted by one of the local Hawaiian gals. The temptation to touch, even stroke, the stunning wall hanging was overwhelming. Lost in thought, she heard a gentle voice behind her say, "OK, you touch."

As Karina strolled over to the next tent, she thought about the quilts and how they would look in a bedroom. It would have to be a large room. Hmmm... someday.

At the back of the next tent, a slight man of Polynesian descent sat on a simple wood stool. The small space was jam-packed with koa bowls, calabashes, and lamp shades. Patches and streaks of gold and yellow competed with highly-polished earthy-browns and tans. The bottoms were handsomely rounded.

The wood turner explained the lengthy process and the scarcity of koa due to logging and the destructive spider mite. Karina fell in love with a small bark-edge koa bowl. She arranged to have it carefully boxed, and then placed in the bottom of her tote-bag.

She wandered through tents of tee-shirts, pareus and muumuus, feathered hats, and hand-made jewelry. Finally, she stopped by the Food Bank, met the volunteers, and then led Sky off in search of the best ice cream. Around her neck hung a polished reddish-brown kukui-nut lei, purchased from one of the talented Hana ladies. She was saving the gifts in her large tote-bag for a special moment.

Carrying cones of heaping taro-kulolo ice cream, they carefully strolled toward their hillside bungalow. Sky's limp added to the challenge of keeping the top scoop from bouncing off.

"I think the best part of the festival was the simplicity," said Karina. "Oh, and the people."

"That and sharing it with you."

"Hmmm, you scored plenty points for that one. Can I get another kiss?"

"Always."

As they neared the edge of the ball field, Sky said, "Look over there. I didn't notice her earlier. See the little gal working at that free massage booth? It's Gecko, one of Rosie's buddies."

"I was just there! I didn't know who she was. I wondered why her questions were so personal. She's got a rough mouth for a little Japanese lady. Strong hands too. It's a benefit booth for something. I gave her a twenty for a ten-minute massage."

"She's nosy all right. She's probably the captain in Rosie's 'slander battalion.' Now you've seen one of the clever disguises of the enemy infiltrators, posing as a tiny Japanese do-gooder."

"To think those little hands were wrapped around my dangling neck," Karina exclaimed with a feigned look of horror — right before she broke out laughing.

Sitting once again on their funky surveillance deck, they reviewed the downside of living in an insidious rumor town. Sky stared straight out, looking particularly concerned. The harsh glare of the afternoon sun deepened his worry lines.

"It's got to be even harder fighting off malicious rumors in this little town, what with everyone knowing everyone. I guess the trick is to get connected with a big support group and have your friends brush off the dirt."

"Did I mention that Dawn is convinced now that she lost her company due to rumors about the business solvency?" Dawn Paris was Karina's confidante and travel companion.

"I heard that she lost a grant over some financial scandal."

"Yeah, and that led to more problems. It was all from baseless gossip."

"I didn't know it was so bad," Sky said, feeling genuine concern. "I'll call her. She's been a friend of mine for a long time."

"She'd like that."

Sky's forehead tightened and his eyes narrowed. "I'll bet she has a damn good idea who perpetrated the rumor."

Driving home in the morning on the canopy-covered highway, they passed through a jungle of monkeypods. With their festive homespun weekend heading into the final leg, Sky felt revved up with appreciation. The award winning Hawaiian trio "Makaha Sons" harmonized from the Jag's dashboard, warm bouquets of tropical aromas drifted across the road, and the spectacularly crooked coastline shored up their romantic notions of life in paradise.

With one hand on the leather steering wheel and one hand on Karina's knee, Sky looked up and shouted at the monkeypods, "Mahalo, Hana!" He turned to Karina and said, "Back to reality."

"Yeah, but remember our reality might be fantasy for others."

ANTONIO'S SALSA

At the Community Center in Kihei, the dial on the air-conditioner was cranked way up for the large crowd of dancers. Antonio, the young dance instructor, was demonstrating the "basic forward" in slow motion. His freewheeling Brazilian torso easily moved through the spicy eight-count. The appreciative groans of the female salsa students were drowned out by the booming Latin music.

"Here's a quick look at salsa," announced Antonio.

Then he sashayed across the stage, highlighting classic Latin twists, pivots, and pulsating energy. Women pondered the possibilities of his limber hips, while men admired how a human body could gyrate with so many quick, contrary moves and not end up in the hospital. The Vixens figured this class would be a good place to meet men with flexibility, rhythm, and stamina.

"He sure has a great butt for such a little guy," whispered Gecko to Rosie.

"Quiet or you'll be up there demonstrating with him," Rosie whispered back.

"You know what he can demonstrate for me," giggled Gecko.

"You guys better shut up or we'll all get in *trouble*," yelled Elizabeth.

Before Liz finished her admonition, the salsa song stopped dead in its track, leaving the word *trouble* hanging in the air, like underwear hanging from a north-Kihei clothesline.

"Join me, señora," commanded Antonio, looking directly into Rosie's eyes. It was clear to Rosie and the two Volcanic Vixens that his request was not open for discussion.

Gecko and Liz started cheering. Soon all 80 students joined the rallying applause for Rosie.

Rosie was slightly shorter than the Brazilian instructor; both wore tight black pants befitting the mood of the hot Latin evening.

"Salsa is about attitude!" yelled Antonio into the portable microphone around his neck, which reverberated around the huge room. "Don't forget the pause! One, two, three — *pause.*"

After seeing Rosie climb onto the stage, the guys along the back wall quickly moved toward the front. Women swarmed to the edge of the stage. Standing nervously near the center of the stage, Rosie took a deep breath.

"This is the close position," said Antonio, with one of those quick Brazilian winks that startle most North American women, but completely elude men. "Framing is important." He pulled Rosie in close with his left hand and with two finger tips of his right hand found the soft spot above her left shoulder blade.

"Don't hold her too tight because her body needs some breathing room — unless you're dirty dancing in a packed club," he quipped, winking once again at the women gathered at the edge of the stage.

He had everyone's attention.

"Lightly touch her right hand and bring your forearm up. And keep it up! Look deep into her eyes with feeling. Remember gentlemen — it's Latin!"

Apprehensively, Rosie lightly touched the crown of his shoulder with three fingers of her left hand. Her right hand eased into the teacher's cupped palm. The students started to understand that salsa was less about direction and more about attitude.

Antonio looked down at Rosie's shapely chest, ignoring her unsteady legs. He intended to sweep her through this dance of passion. Rosie inhaled deeply, shrinking the distance between them. Liz crossed her fingers, feeling guilty over her untimely outburst, while Gecko licked her lips in anticipation.

The instructor led Rosie through a series of seductive salsa steps with a "spaghetti-arm" flurry. As the Latin beat began to sear through their pores, he skillfully guided her through a number of undulating motions, like a snake charmer working his cobra. The final sequence ended with a dramatic "drop neck" dip that bent Rosie's spine backwards, her head hovering just above the stage floor. Wide-eyed, every student in the room burst into applause.

"Hana hou!" yelled a few guys above the cheers.

Looking incredulous as she left the stage, Rosie was astounded that she could be led through all those maneuvers without prior instruction.

"Bravo, señora!" applauded Liz as Rosie returned. "You gave a pretty sexy performance considering you've got 20 years on him. You could be his *mother*. Maybe you got some Brazilian blood."

"You're *only* two years younger than me, Liz. You could be his mama too."

"Hey, I'm only 12 years older than that hot

"chimichanga," said Gecko. "I could be his sexy sister." Rosie and Liz looked at their little Japanese friend and broke out laughing.

Later that night at Tommy's, Rosie's maiden dance was critiqued and toasted by her pals with potent "Bahama Blasts."

Overhead candelabras, wrapped in large baskets of seashells, illuminated the lounge. The décor was extensive bamboo with an assortment of natural cane delicately balancing heavy teak and mahogany. The trio of salsa-dancing Vixens settled in a corner table, choosing vintage fabric chairs to decompress from the steamy class.

"Let's hear about your 'free lesson' with Señor Brazil," said Liz. "That was quick of him slipping his phone number to you with a Thursday night question mark."

"He's cute, isn't he?" asked Rosie coyly.

"He's cute all right!" exclaimed Gecko. "How about you give me Antonio's phone number, and I'll give you a dozen massages."

"Save your freebies. You can be his dance puppet next week. I have my church group on Thursdays. I haven't missed a meeting in three years, and I'm *not* starting now. Of course, there's something to be said about a chance to nibble on that gyrating South American butt. Hmmm... maybe another time. Shit, he's just a poor young dancer in search of a green card."

"All this salsa stuff has given me an idea," said Liz. "Let's have a party at my house. I'll supply everything, including your companions. Giorgio's can cater. What do you think?"

"I love it!" yelled Gecko, quickly realizing her volume carried the length of the lounge.

"It sounds perfect," said Rosie, "I'll check my week-at-a-glance."

"These dance classes are a primer on who's doing who, and who's on the loose," noted Liz. "These couples change their partners more often than I change my hair. Too bad the guys are flush from being the 'dumper' or the 'dumpee.'"

"Yeah, too bad," said Gecko. "What they need is a little physical therapy to get them out of their funk."

"Some of us need serious time to get over abusive relationships!" exploded Rosie. There was silence for a few seconds as Liz and Gecko realized the hurt that Rosie was still experiencing.

"Meaning?" asked Liz.

"Meaning Sky slapped me around during our last month together. Not to mention the affair with that woman."

"Shit! We had no idea it was that bad," said Liz. "You should have told us right away."

"I'm sorry too," said Gecko, "but it was a long time ago."

Liz and Gecko looked at each other, avoiding Rosie's eyes for the moment and wondering where this conversation was headed.

"You've had a lot of bad luck with men," said Liz. "Especially since your last two husbands had the audacity to get killed *after* you left them."

"Yeah," said Gecko, "at least you scored big time from your first husband's sudden death."

"They were all jerks, but men like Sky should be exterminated!" exclaimed Rosie.

"I'll call the bug man in the morning," kidded Gecko, breaking into a braying laughter.

"Good thing I didn't see Sky on the dance floor

tonight, because I'm not through with him!" warned Rosie, gritting her teeth. Her pals stared at her for a while, waiting for her next response.

"Now I want another toast to the sexiest salsa dancer to ever hit the stage, if I do say so myself," proclaimed Rosie, suddenly smiling. She raised her Bahama Blast and clinked glasses with her Vixen buddies.

"And a toast to the only loose-hipped Asian on the floor who knows how to shake it," declared Gecko, breaking into another round of laughter.

"Loose all right," teased Liz, sneaking a peak at her watch.

"Some of us have early morning jobs," said Rosie. "It's been fun. See you kids later."

"Ciao, everyone," said Liz.

"I'll wait five minutes to see if the hunk at the bar knows how to offer a shy Japanese goddess a drink," said Gecko. Everyone laughed as Rosie and Liz started to head home.

WHALE BLOWS

The sparkling clear water lapped at the "Wailea Warrior," a 42-foot whale-watch catamaran. It was idling two miles off the coast of Maui, between McGregor Point and the snorkeling mecca of Molokini. Only the deep purr of the engine could be heard. The tourists, locals, and crew on board were mesmerized as a pod of humpback whales headed directly toward them across the silky sea.

"One o'clock," sounded a deep voice from the top deck.

"And closing fast," added a young woman standing on the bow. Her rapid, high-pitched announcement suggested fear.

The last of the five hyperactive whales "waved" its tail to the passengers as if to say goodbye, right before it disappeared with a graceful dive.

"Where are they, mommy?" asked a small boy clinging tight to his mother's leg.

"The calm before the storm," whispered Sky to Karina.

Everyone on the boat watched anxiously for the reappearance of the ocean giants. Suddenly Karina cried out, "They're coming right at us!"

Cameras ready, the spectators watched the

surface of the ocean change from a warm translucent blue to a bone-chilling black. Dark water spread out in front of the motionless boat.

Sky wrapped his arm around Karina's shoulder in a protective hold, and they both braced against the wheelhouse wall. He kissed her quickly.

The sea exploded off the port bow as a new mother rocketed skyward in a powerful booming breach. Passengers screamed as the 45-ton acrobatic beauty rose completely above her salty sanctuary.

Mama arched over in an airborne pirouette, and with a lurching twist, landed on her dorsal side with a dead-flat landing. She crashed into the calm water with an earsplitting crack that could be heard for miles around. The splash sprayed everyone on the bow. Shielding Karina from the sea shower, Sky asked, "Was that close enough?"

Even before the excited screams faded, there was a thud astern. The rear of the boat lifted up, pitching three tourists across the black canvas spray-guard and into the sea. Two of them were exotic dancers from the famous Pussycat Lounge in Honolulu. They tumbled awkwardly into the water off the port bow without the slightest regard for aerial style.

On the other hand, the unintended flight of the newlywed computer programmer was far more visually artistic. His launch gave him enough momentum to complete a full somersault before landing in the water. The tourists on the upper deck were in total disarray, or they would have given him a high score for creative artistry — with a small deduction for his splash.

"Oh, no," gasped Karina, "do something!"

"I would, but there's already plenty of help."

Luckily the boat was still idling on the gentle ocean. Every guy on the bow deck raced forward to help pull up the women, who were treading water alongside the hull.

Hoisting the bikini-clad women was tricky, because they had slathered their young flesh with an oily sunscreen. There were very few places for the guys to grab; they were either too slippery or too personal.

"Looks like pulling half-frozen fish from a barrel of ice," kidded Sky.

The programmer swam to the rescue and pushed the women up with a strong hand to their shapely rumps. His new wife was not as impressed as the rest of the tourists, who were cheering in appreciation of the sea rescue.

The underwater bump had been caused by humpback whale "challengers" fighting to outmaneuver the male escort in hopes of having a shot at mating. They were using head slams, fluke slaps, glancing head rams, and tactical dives.

"One of the giants got flipped around in the battle and forgot about our boat," said Sky. "Hope the hull survived OK."

"What's next?" asked Karina, clinging to her lover and the railing at the same time.

"I think the show's over. Let's get a couple of mai tais and make sure they're heavy on the rum. Whale watching doesn't get better than that. Watching the challengers jostling for escort position was worth 20 bucks, but watching those guys jostling for hero status was worth even more."

"I was scared the boat would flip. I'll be diving off my bed from nightmares tonight."

A pungent odor of rotten fish had infiltrated

the catamaran. It smelled more like a returning fishing vessel than a sightseeing boat, the result of the baleen blows. The active pod had been breathing faster than normal, and the lingering stink from the 200 mile-per-hour "geyser exhaust" was a reminder of the violent drama.

Karina was bursting with excitement. "What a battle! And we were on the frontline. The breaches were unreal, especially the baby arching completely above the water. You'd think they were launching from underwater trampolines."

"I know," said Sky. "Hard to believe it's just two fluke flicks before they're airborne. The mom was probably using our boat as a protective buffer from all that aggressive blubber when she breached."

"It's not easy being a mom in these waters. Bringing up a newborn with males fighting over you and trying to screw you has to be a tough job. Kind of like some human behavior."

"That's for sure. Some of their aggressive actions are far more similar to ours than you can imagine," said Sky, suddenly unable to look into Karina's eyes. His words became softer and he turned his face.

The cabin was packed. Everyone was drinking up the liquor as fast as the bar boys could prepare the tropicals. Yoshio, the naturalist, had worked his way over to the central life preserver box, where there was an animated group of rum guzzlers. Yoshio exclaimed, "You see it? I never see before!"

"See them? We felt them and we smelled them," yelled Sky above the roar of the boat's droning clamor and loud chatter from the crowded cabin. "You got that kind of whale action off the coast of Japan?"

"No, no! Not fighting too much. We lucky today.

Now you tell friends about it."

"We will. Thanks for the show," shouted Karina.

"Yeah, thanks Yoshio. Maybe next week you can arrange something a little more exciting," added Sky with a big smile. He lifted his plastic glass. "Banzai!" The cabin erupted in toasts of "banzai."

The sun had set by the time they walked up to the deck. The tourist boat was rapidly approaching the harbor. Everyone was clapping loudly as they glided past the protective rock jetties, including Captain Dan, who glanced over at his slip and thought it had never looked lovelier.

Night quickly descended on Ma'alaea, and a magenta haze settled across the West Maui Mountains. The high peaks and the drifting clouds blocked out the last light of the day. Cheery harbor lights welcomed the boisterous boatload of whale-watching neophytes, already exaggerating their sea stories.

The two humpback enthusiasts walked over to the Blue Marlin lounge. There wasn't a car in sight when Karina suddenly halted in the middle of the harbor road and gave Sky a long passionate kiss. Their public behavior looked like a lascivious French couple to the Blue Marlin lounge lizards sitting at their view tables. This afternoon marked their third whale adventure together, and every outing had been a different cetacean song and dance performance.

Over deep-fried calamari strips, chicken-wing pupu, and white wine, Karina said, "I loved the first three whales we saw. I can't believe the mother was floating with her calf cradled across the bump on her head. Then the escort gave the baby the same free ride and the mom allowed it. Wow!"

67

"Captain Dan said he had never seen a mother give up her kid to another whale for even a second," added Sky, remembering the emotional outburst from the old sea veteran standing on the bridge.

"Nice to see some male nurturing for a change," said Karina, equally amazed at the tenderness of the escort. "I always miss these big playful characters when they leave in May. I feel a spiritual connection with them. We're lucky they choose our home to procreate and nurture. Now they're about to break my heart again and head back to Alaska."

"I feel the same way, kitten, but they have to end their fast and get back for a real dinner. I'm sad, too, when they head to the mainland. On the other hand, when my 'snowbird' friends leave Maui for their frigid North American nests, I'm usually relieved."

"It's touching that some of local researchers call our humpbacks, 'Kama'aina whales.' This *is* their birthplace after all. Cheers, sweetie!"

"Banzai!"

ULUPALAKUA THING

Purple lilies of the Nile framed the strategic, triangular upcountry junction. Four magnificent jacaranda trees, their leaves transformed into blazing purple, thrived inside the flower-lined triangle. Anyone not making a left turn toward Haleakala on this late-April Saturday morning was going straight to the Maui Agricultural Trade Show and Tasting at Ulupalakua Ranch and Tedeschi Vineyards — the "Ulupalakua Thing." Sky aimed the Jaguar straight ahead.

"Half the island should be there, Ms. Karina. Seven-thousand natives will be stampeding the ranch looking for parking. Good thing we're VIPs today. Gets us inside an hour early before all the vultures crawl out of their sweaty beach condos and flock to this cool air.

"It's an agricultural show, Maui style, which means lots of free food samples for the early birds. Best feast of the year for an eight-dollar ticket. And you can see why they call it the *Thing*. It's more than an AG show with all the music, celebrity chef cook-offs, and the ambience of the Tedeschi Winery gardens. It's kind of a community social featuring Maui-made products. You'll like the looks of the hunky paniolos directing traffic."

"Well then, let's giddyap."

After the jacaranda tree quartet, the rolling, bright-green countryside was rampant with purple. Bougainvillea competed with jacarandas, which were showing off their finest glory in a panoramic blaze of color. Alongside the jacarandas, silky oaks displayed their own golden "thing."

"There's a great view of Haleakala," she gasped. "Pull over so I can take a photo. Look how the horses add to the country charm. They kind of put our big mountain of spiritual energy into perspective."

"You're right about the energy. Most folks don't realize that she's not an extinct volcano. She's only resting from her latest lava discharge. Technically she's an active volcano."

"What! What recent lava flow?"

"Apparently you were on vacation last year. Sorry, just kidding. Nobody knows exactly. Very little research has been done on the Maui calderas. The best guess is two to six hundred-years-ago, which still classifies her as active. The last eruption took place a few miles past the winery. That's the lava flow that made it all the way to the ocean at Makena."

"But, it's so peaceful here."

"The big question is whether she's still in a 'rejuvenation stage.' Anyway, remind me not to buy any ranch land past Ulupalakua or acreage down in Makena. Not much value in owning a hot imu pit or a pointy cinder cone."

"Thanks for the warning. I've always felt the energy of this mountain. There's more power and magic here than I can describe."

"I think I know what you're feeling," Sky mused, pausing for a moment and staring toward the peak with appreciation and awe.

Sky loved playing tour guide for Karina because it brought out her youthful enthusiasm. She had been on the island for only a couple of years, and there was a world of hidden island treasures waiting for her.

"Look the other way," he said. "You get a sense of the entire shape of Maui. It's an *isthmus*. There's the ocean on both sides of the valley, and Mauna Kahalawai rising from the valley floor. There's something sexy about the curvy narrow-waist outline of the two coasts. And those mysterious 'Teton' peaks are constantly changing moods."

"Is this your Scorpio side conjuring up another perverted apparition?"

"Probably."

Just past Grandma's Coffee House they drove across the cattle ranch lands of Ulupalakua. The appearance of the small boomerang island of Molokini had become an undistinguished blob.

Neighbor islands not only changed shape, but seemed to shift their alignment depending on one's vantage point. The bomb-ridden island of Kahoʻolawe dominated their immediate view, almost completely crowned by great patches of terra-cotta colors across its eastern slopes. It was especially bright with the intense morning sun highlighting the firebrick-red clay and creeping into the wrinkled crevices of the steep black cliffs.

The former pineapple island of Lanaʻi was a distant one-dimensional blur in the background, and Molokaʻi was hidden behind the sexy West Maui Mountains.

Once they reached the winery on the ranch, they followed the paniolos to a dusty parking place.

An enormous, stately camphor tree offered a cool canopy of shade across most of the winery grounds. After their names were checked, they entered through a makeshift gate.

"Let's graze this morning on all the free samples, and if we still have room there's a lunch roasting on those giant spits," Sky suggested. "I have to find Buddy. He's working at his friend's 'Paia Fudge' booth.

"Ah! There he is, talking to one of the girls at the 'Lavender Scents' stall. Oh *yeah*. He's busy rustling up a sweet-smelling companion for the evening."

Buddy Kanoa had been his pal for 15 years. They had been joint owners of a dive boat years ago and often shared in outdoor adventures. Buddy was a pig hunter, boat captain, and roustabout ladies man. Even with his heavy frame he was known to be as light as a floating feather on the ballroom dance floor.

He was standing in front of the scent tent, navigating his infamous Captain Charm role with a delightfully endowed, purple-wigged salesgirl named Joni. Buddy was sipping the popular "Lavender Lemonade," a heavenly drink, whose taste lingers for a while on the forefront of the tongue.

"Eh, Sky; eh, Karina. I gonna see ya at dat fudge booth."

He quickly jotted down Joni's phone number and confirmed a private sunset cruise on his multi-purpose charter boat. With the demeanor of a luxury cruise ship captain, he presented her with his embossed "Runs with Spinners" social card, referring to both his fishing lures and to the high-flying dolphins that occasionally escorted his boat.

Joni had the face of a librarian and the body of a stripper. The purple-haired salesgirl enthusiastically accepted Buddy's Saturday night proposal, although she was unsure as to the meaning "Runs with Spinners," typed in large blue print across his social card. It brought back memories of her promiscuous sorority days. Ironically, Spinner was her nickname in college earned from her acrobatic sexual maneuvers.

"Howzit, Karina?" Buddy asked back at the fudge booth, bypassing her right cheek and planting a wet kiss dead center on her lips. Close friends in this circle greeted each other with full-on lip kisses, not lengthy, but occasionally juicy.

"Eh, Brah, you and yer sweet lady gotta try dis new mango-fudge concoction. Some plenty ono. I t'ink so all pau by noon. Lucky you early."

Buddy paused for a second and then blurted, "So what's up wit' da rumors 'bout you and dat Portagee woman when you still wit' Rosie?" Karina stood in silence.

"Where did you hear that?"

"One of my tango chicks at practice tell me. Who knows where she hear it. She shocked me and I jus' tell her I hope it wasn't wit' ma sista. I was jus' kiddin'. Maybe she don't know I like kid around."

Buddy Kanoa often assumed the ethnic identity befitting his situation. Under his broad shoulders were the souls of many of the island's ethnic blends. In truth, he was part of the largest group, "mixed plate local," or "hapa." Impersonating Portuguese descent at this moment was as conceivable for him as claiming a limb on any of the island family tree, including Hawaiian, Filipino, Japanese, Mexican, Chinese, Samoan or haole.

Purebloods on this isolated Polynesian rock were in a small minority. Most islanders were homespun hybrids sharing a small incestuous spit of land in the middle of the great Pacific Ocean. No matter the group, Buddy fit right in.

"Gee, thanks for perpetuating that disgusting rumor," said Sky. "Explain to Karina that despite all the lovely Portuguese women on the island, I don't personally know any. That includes your lovely sister, who by the way is hardly Portuguese.

"Seriously, this is all *crap*. It's not fair to Karina either. Hopefully you don't believe any of this, kitten?"

"Well, you are pretty cute."

"Very *funny*. So much for having friends defend my honor. Buddy, is our pig hunt still on for next month?"

"You bet. Da dogs gettin' real antsy. Dey like hunt already. And t'inkin 'bout dat hunt now makin' me hungry. Time for go buffalo-chili tent and get da bison burger and onion rings. I gonna get one pink, 50-gallon, Styrofoam, cowboy hat on da way. No respectable pig hunter like to be caught dead wit'out one."

"If we see you wearing it, please don't act like you know us," teased Karina.

"Sky, I need one word wit' you in da back."

"Sure."

"I'll wander around," said Karina.

Behind the tent, Buddy whispered into Sky's ear, "Eh, da odda t'ing goin' 'round is you wen take Rosie's necklaces. I heard cost plenty money. Maybe mo' bullshit, but you should know what da stink is."

Sky exploded with pent-up frustration. "Damn it! You got it right when you said 'bullshit.' I'm choosing to ignore it all. Let's remember the source.

And let's remember the *last* time I chose to defend someone. Cost me three years in jail saving that druggie from getting beat to death by her boyfriend!"

"She one bad woman, maybe she dead now. She lied in court like it gospel, but you had to help dat woman. Was plenty long time back for you."

"Twenty years, but the memory is like yesterday." Unknowingly, Sky had his right fist clenched while he recalled that awful time in his life. "Slamming each other into that wall. I still have this damn limp from breaking my leg, and not getting it fixed right in jail. Jesus, Buddy, you know he would have killed me if he didn't crack his head on that pole."

"I know. No fault you. Now you jus' be careful."

"Yeah, I've been careful. Because of those two women, I've spent a lot of years being careful.

Later while waiting in a long line at the popular "Susie's Ono Won Tons" tent, Sky exclaimed, "Oh, shit! Rosie and that socialite bitch are coming through the gate. I wondered why my ears were burning.

"The problem with these events is there's no gate to screen out terroristic trash mouths. If I have to introduce you, you're banned from spending even two minutes alone with that twisted fibber. Hopefully we won't see them again in this large crowd."

"It would be fun to talk story with your former friend over tea now that I know her so well," said Karina with a wink. "I might get some useful information."

"More like disinformation!" Sky growled. "If I had any more supportive friends like you and Buddy, I might as well join a Sufi commune." He reached for a small cup of spicy Thai sauce to dip his won tons in.

Sharp-eyed Elizabeth Brinkley had spotted the

sea life artist and his new girlfriend. Liz was Rosie's best buddy and confidante. They shared the belief that the greatest pastime in life was chatting about other people. Gossip was the glue that bonded them.

"Rosie, there's your old pal, Sky, with his new honey. Can you handle a confrontation?"

"When have I *ever* lost my composure?" asked Rosie. "But forget him; I'm more excited about seeing my cowboy buddies again. I did vet work on some of the Ulupalakua Ranch cattle recently.

"Funny though, that skinny bitch looks familiar. Sky never had a lot of down time after the death of a relationship, especially with his overworked, indiscriminate sex drive. Anyway, let's see if we can get a Kula salad or maybe something sweet. My blood sugar needs a boost."

Liz Brinkley was the envy of the Volcanic Vixens. She had a pricey home in Makena and was one of the wealthiest residents in the area. She wore her blond hair short; her wrinkle-free face featured thin lips and dark eyebrows. Regular workouts and a picky appetite kept her tall figure thin. She dabbled with real estate investments, but it was more to occupy her time than to add to her net worth.

Liz had known her veterinarian friend for years. Rosie had saved her champion Chihuahua "Cashew" from an epileptic seizure. The applehead pedigree had banged her soft scull on the lanai railing chasing after a pesky mynah bird. The two women became friends during the recovery of the little yipper.

For the next hour everyone enjoyed peace and harmony wandering around the winery gardens, along with thousands of happy gluttons sampling fruit spreads, salads, and desserts. Suddenly, while waiting in the lamb shish-kebab line, Sky was poked sharply in the back.

"You *better* watch your back," Rosie hissed through her teeth."

Turning around and ignoring the painful jab, Sky said pleasantly, "Hello, Rosie, Liz." Have you met my friend, Karina?"

"No, I haven't," said Rosie. "It's nice to meet you. Wait a minute! You *are* the same one. From the pygmy rescue. It's *very* nice to see you again, Karina. This is my friend, Liz."

"It's a pleasure, Liz," said Karina. "And it's good to see you under better circumstances, Rosie."

Rosie said, "Yes... well, what a great party. We've been snacking all morning. I was just talking to a couple of pals from the ranch here and they have two sick heifers they want me to reexamine. The cattle up here are having some digestive problems from the lack of grass. This drought is taking a toll throughout the area. Hey, the shish kebabs look great. Is everyone getting the deluxe ones with the Kula onions and tomatoes?"

Rosie was simply being her lovable, professional, and chatty self. Liz was disappointed that there weren't any fireworks, no barbs slung back and forth by the former couple, no catfight between Sky's girlfriends, past or present.

Karina, on the other hand, was impressed that Rosie was still the friendly, caring person she knew from the whale rescue. Sky was thinking about where he wanted to stick his skewer after chewing off the ingredients.

"Yeah," said Sky in a cheerful tone. "We're taking a couple of extra skewers for a picnic later," hoping his words hid his anger. "It's nice to see you both." They all parted after pleasant farewells.

As they headed back to the Jag, Karina noticed some smoke rising over the crater. "Hey, looks like some steam on top," she exclaimed, quickly turning to him.

"Sorry," Sky apologized. "I shouldn't have talked about the possibility of an eruption. Those are thermal clouds that rise up from the crater and drift down to Wailea in the afternoon.

"Besides, Haleakala is not the kind of volcano that's likely to blow, although it's possible that it could erupt if enough water got into a vent. This type of volcano is more likely to have a smaller eruption and spew lava at a slower pace. That's why it has that smooth tapered shape.

"Speaking of blowing your top," he continued, "I was glad that Rosie didn't erupt. In public she has that sweet professional personality. Who's going to think she has a twisted side?"

"She's actually very nice. I'm always reading about her saving whales, or horses, or feral cats, or something. She seems smart too. Don't vets go to school longer than an MD?"

Exasperated, he responded, "I think they do. She's been a vet on the island for a long time. Her reputation makes it easy for people to swallow her bullshit."

"Actually, I found Liz more interesting, dressed in her beaded cowgirl outfit. I'm guessing that she's worth a few rhinestones."

"That's for sure. She has a few expensive homes scattered around Wailea."

"So tell me, what's this surprise picnic you have planned?"

"You'll see. Do I need to blindfold you before you see those paniolos again?"

"You know you're the only cowboy in my life. Especially since you're packing shish kebabs and chilled champagne in those saddlebags."

"Be nice to me, Pancho, because I know where there's a nice patch of cactus waiting for your tender butt."

PRICKLY AFFAIR

After driving a few miles from the event, the last point of reference for Karina was passing the Temple Dog Park. Then it was a big blur of twisty curves and turns.

Sky's picnic place measured up to its reticent billing. The view was a visual panoramic banquet — extraordinaire. Spread out before them was a delectable smorgasbord. Rows of verdant, silver-jade pineapple appeared as one great salad bowl in the center of the panorama. From the west coast, rising waves of headlands appeared as clusters of whipped, chocolate frosting and goldenrod custards.

With the view whetting her lips, Karina devoured the master's canvas. "I'm visualizing hills of butterscotch and saucers of flan."

"You're right. I see kiwi-colored forests and mounds of Key lime sorbet smack in the middle."

Finishing her second glass of champagne, she exclaimed, "Oh, and maybe scoops of chocolate mocha near the top. I must be preoccupied with food from all the goodies we saw earlier."

"You should paint landscapes, with your imagination," said Sky.

"Thanks, but I'll leave the oils to you," she

replied, suddenly thinking of her home country and the secret she harbored.

Karina was terrified that Sky would find out that she had a husband in Norway. Her husband had assured her that the divorce papers would soon be final. There had never been an urgency to divorce after they parted amicably many years ago. Karina now had a tall, dark, and lovable reason for quick legal closure. Unfortunately the paperwork dragged on. She also realized that this dilemma provided a convenient reason to avoid thinking about making a lifetime commitment to Sky. She knew she wasn't ready.

Sky poured more sparkling wine. The view and their appetites joined forces. Puffs of floating cotton candy hovered over the emerald peaks. They spread out their picnic using three beach mats as a portable table.

Karina leaned back on her forearms against the slight rise of the small grassy knoll, surrounded by rocks and boulders. It was late in the afternoon and the vanilla cumulus over the ocean horizon held promise of a memorable sunset.

"I love your cute harness that holds the champagne bottle," she said. "Keeps it chilled and handy to pour. Simple. Just like your spot here. Nothing around except that delicious view, lots of cactus that look like bunny ears, and a few castor bean plants. It's so quiet I hesitate to spoil it — even with a whisper."

"A few cattle in the area, but that's about the extent of it." He leaned back on the adjacent beach mat and spoke with the fervor of a tour guide.

"It's simple, peaceful nature, along with the perfect climate. Did you know the year-round temperature here at 2500-feet elevation has been rated the best livable climate in the world? I have to agree. The air is so crisp."

"It's very romantic here, angel. I'm always impressed with your secret places, but I have to admit this one's the best. And the little chunks of roasted lamb go perfectly with your terrace setting. Can you pour some more bubbly?

"I've been wondering. You don't think Buddy could be the culprit who started the rumors?"

"Hell no! I've known him for 15 years. He gets things messed up once in a while, but he would never intentionally harm me. Besides, Rosie has a history of trash talking about her ex-husbands. I often worried she would turn on me if something happened between us."

"What did happen?" asked Karina. "You've never told me."

"The reasons are fuzzy, but her behavior totally changed the last couple of months we were together. It got spooky after awhile. She became nasty and physically aggressive. Toward the end she seemed to have an altered state of mind.

"One of the reasons that I hung on was her weird history and the untimely demise of her last two husbands. They were both dead within two years of the divorce. I'm not superstitious, but I didn't want to find myself in the Maui News obits. Aren't you glad you brought this up?"

"Actually, I am. I believe her sour grapes allowed our love affair to blossom quicker. This afternoon was a great example of the fun we have together. But, Jesus! What did happen to those guys?"

"Freaky accidents. One got run over by a truck

and the other fell out of a kayak in the middle of the night. Let's change the subject because right now I'm thinking about that view and how the light is seeping into your skin. Cheers! To a perfect day."

"Cheers, my special one."

Soon, the ocean swallowed up the last image of bulbous light. They finished off the heavy pupu and were sipping the last glass of champagne. It was getting dark around their rocky and thorny panoramic perch.

The gentle, fading light caressed their passions and ignited their desire for each other. Karina quivered in lust as Sky's smoldering gaze stoked her body. They craved physical passion; the freedom of the open air offered innocence.

Urgently, he set his glass down and lightly brushed her neck. Two fingers traced the ridge of her spine from her slender nape down to her denim shorts. Because of the sensory overload surrounding the picnic knoll, it took only seconds before shirts and shorts were tossed aside. Suddenly, they were as naked as the prickly pear.

Their craving had to harmonize with the retreating sunlight. They made it intense, even animalistic. Due to the cool air and the sudden encounter, they were laying on a mat without a bead of sweat on their naked bodies.

"Wow! What the hell is that?" Sky exclaimed, as a chill raced down his spine. "Someone there?"

They could see movement in the dim twilight above their knoll. In fact, they could see lots of movement.

"Jesus! It's a bunch of cows coming down. Man, they're close! I wonder if we're on their path. Shit! They're not stopping!"

"Sky, let's move! Right *now*! There's so many. Wait! It looks like they're slowing down. They're just standing around watching us. You know, maybe they expect us to feed them. Maybe they're not out to trample us."

"How strange. Maybe Rosie's up there stampeding them," he joked. They listened to a car drive down the desolate road.

"Nah, let's not let our imaginations go wild over a few friendly cows," she said.

"Right. Curious cows, looking for a handout. Looks like it's time to abandon our cattle fort and head back before it's too dark to see the lava shards in this clumpy grass. Not to mention the spiky balloon plants and our prickly cactus buddies lurking all over the place. I think we're out of our element up here, Pancho. Next time I'll bring a cattle prod," he laughed.

"You'd better — at least a cow whistle."

VENOMOUS CHARGES

"Did you see that?" yelled Sky, jumping to his feet.

"I saw something flash by, a streak of color." Karina tried to straighten her curled legs.

It was a particularly beautiful pre-summer afternoon, which was common on Maui. The "snowbirds" and high rollers had left and the summer invasion of families was yet to be seen. It was one of the tranquil off-season periods when residents caught their breath and recharged their spirit of aloha. Sky and Karina were relaxing in Sky's African living room.

"Maybe it's some kind of lizard," said Sky walking toward the Kalahari corner of the living room, where a small herd of carved zebras were milling about. "Oh shit, it's a centipede! How the hell did it get in here?"

"It's the tropics, baby. I'll get the roach can," said Karina. She headed toward the "bug-war pantry," where an arsenal of weapons was stockpiled to combat invasions of small animals, large insects, and scary looking tropical pests. Only the comical and beneficial gecko was exonerated.

Sky looked around for something to deal with the dangerous intruder. He remembered Buddy talking about grabbing one of the critters with BBQ tongs. He rushed to find a long-handled one. When he returned, Karina was crouched down attempting to shoot the wriggling centipede with roach spray. The flashy party crasher tried to blend behind a baby zebra leg, a poor choice for his glossy reddish-brown hide. The spraying infuriated him.

"Back off, back off!" yelled Sky. "They're so fast they can practically fly at you." Karina jumped back halfway across the room. The cornered myriapod reared its ugly head and pointed his front pair of poisonous fangs toward Sky's face.

"Careful! You'll be in the hospital if he bites," warned Karina as she left the room. Sky maneuvered into a favorable battle position.

With its potentially lethal poison, the centipede raised its head again as Karina reappeared. As the combatant poised to charge, Karina blasted away with a fire extinguisher, and the poisonous pest vanished in a sea of chemical foam. Sky's hardwood floor would need refinishing.

"Well, that sure extinguished the danger." said Sky. "I could have used your help when a Cape buffalo charged our van in Tanzania."

"My pleasure. I didn't like the direction of those fangs." Giggling, she said, "just protecting the family jewels. I'll get the broom and dust pan."

"Thanks. I'll get the mop and the champagne. After we clean up, let's move up to the top deck." He gave her a warm hug. Karina wondered if Rosie still had a key to his house.

Later, Karina stood next to the privacy railing, resting on her slim forearms. The ocean view was extraordinary. Sky had designed the large observation deck so that it snuggled up to his roofline, unnoticed in the highly regulated Wailea neighborhood. The platform had exceptional views of the sea and mountains. A small corner bar kept the ambience intimate, and the cushioned lounge chairs were positioned for stargazing.

Sky cut a handsome figure as he crossed the deck with a couple of skinny champagne flutes filled with bubbles. The delicate glass stems featured whimsical red hearts, suggesting to Karina either the owner's feminine side or a gift from a female friend. Sky's long stride made short work of the extensive Mexican-tiled deck.

"I always read stories about the beauty of paradise, but never fully imagined it," said Karina. "There's something about the sounds and smells that complete the picture."

"I usually give my mainland friends the island's downside," joked Sky. "Keeps them home and shortens the lines here." A Hawaiian song with a bluesy beat started playing from the bar radio.

"That's the 'Hana Boys'," said Karina. "Remember them from the Taro Festival? They came to Local Style a few times and put some blues into their Hawaiian renditions. They were a big hit at the club, and already they're out with a record."

"Great sound. Lucky they met one of the island's movers and shakers."

"That's what my club is all about; giving local groups a jumpstart, especially if they can mix it up with our blues and jazz theme. Well, that and making money. The place is packed every night."

"You've got the right touch," said Sky. "Now, don't even say it. I have to get down there more often."

The last tip of the setting sun presented a small, but genuine green flash. The sunset beckoned applause, and with chilled brut in hand they toasted the end of the day. Twilight pastel clouds raced across the top of the West Maui Mountains. The vaporous clouds disappeared after rolling across the warm Pacific waters. Pungent night-blooming jasmine started to seep through the deck.

Karina dreaded telling Sky about the latest accusation. "Sweetie, there's another rumor. Supposedly, you have Rosie's collection of expensive Kenyan necklaces hidden away somewhere."

"Wow! She's full of surprises. I wonder why she's making this stuff up now. She's never called about this, and I've never seen her necklaces, if they even exist. I love African art, but I already have my own collection."

"I know, I know! It's weird she's doing this. You should do something."

"What can I do? Calling her would lead to a tirade. The problem is that I get this crap second hand. I'll tell you what I plan to do. Nothing! I'm a lover, not a fighter. Besides, my reputation should satisfy anyone's doubts." Then he remembered that, at one time, long ago, he was a fighter.

"I totally believe you," said Karina. "Rosie's obviously holding some kind of grudge. But maybe you should consider dealing with it in some way."

"Maybe I will at some point, but let me ask you this. How do we know when neurotic behavior has slipped over the dark edge?"

"I'm not sure what you mean," said Karina.

Sky continued into uncharted territory. "If we see mean-spirited behavior, how can we tell if it's coming from a character flaw or a real demented mind? I'm beginning to have serious questions about Rosie's mental state."

The softening of the evening sky and the merging of the intense sunset colors were ignored as he continued. "Are there definitive red flags for psychosis? Before someone significant moves into your life, it seems to me that they should be required to hand over a list of warning signs."

Karina watched him become as intense as the twilight colors. She knew he was passionate about art and lovemaking, but he had always kept his innermost feelings to himself.

"It seems to me that we would have a natural instinct regarding the stability of our mate, especially with enough time spent...."

"After a relationship is long over, there should be a gag order on someone insane," he growled. "Shouldn't we be able to muzzle the culprit and tie the scumbag to a public post? The trouble is that a small community relishes hearing about sex and scandal." He started to smile again as he realized that rumors on a small island were part of the package of living in paradise.

"Maybe I should make up something about her. But what? Her status in the community makes her invincible. Hell, I refuse to play her game. Besides, I'm busy teaming up with a sexy slayer of poisonous vermin."

"What about starting a rumor that she had a hand in the death of all her husbands? We know that she pushed one over the edge."

"Wow! You play hardball. Actually there's always been talk about that, more like quiet whispers than blatant rumors. Maybe I should kick them into high gear."

"You couldn't do that."

"I know."

He wandered off to grab the rest of the Korbel, and tried to corral his emotions during the champagne trek. Since hearing the bogus gossip, his attitude had switched from farcical amusement to fear that a former lover could have been a live-in lunatic. By choosing the button-pushing rumors of infidelity and thievery, he realized that she had declared all-out war.

Karina watched Sky's frustration with concern. She worried that all this might put their relationship on hold. On his return she flipped her long red hair back and gave him a teasing smile. She was ready to take on his emotional outpourings. In the last couple of months, they had become each other's best coach. Now it was her turn to rally the team.

Reaching for her fresh glass, she coyly tested his mood. "Angel, we must always remember one thing: Sky's the limit." Seeing a smile, she continued. "Maybe you're a closet psychiatrist ready to delve into the recesses of the fickle female mind. Any training in the human psyche?"

"A few psych classes. I still use the old behavioral terms when I'm joking around with some of my neurotic friends. You know, like projection, fetishism, and my favorite one — wacko.

"But seriously, there must be a way to identify the potential for psychotic behavior in the beginning of a relationship. This is more than a sour grapes reaction to my walking out on that woman."

Karina knew that a long night of lovemaking would soon be the best cure for both of their frustrations. She watched the first planet appear, just over the sparkling ocean horizon. Probably Venus, she thought, sitting on the rattan barstool near the edge of the sky deck. To change the mood, she said,

"Think about where we are."
"True. No other place like it."

HIGH NOON AT SAFEWAY

Karina Johnsen woke up to an odd smell, a burning smell. She had been looking forward to this Saturday morning all week long. It was already warm outside; early-summer heat offering a preview of the new season.

She had planned a long-overdue weekend of personal pampering, and today's prescription called for a full dose of self-indulgence. Her schedule noted: read a romantic novel at the beach in the morning, shop in the early afternoon, long nap, and happy-hour drinks with Sky at five. Tomorrow would be the ultimate in pampering with a four-hour deluxe spa and massage combo at the Grand Wailea Resort. Dawn Paris would join her for the splurge.

After brushing the sleep from her eyes, she walked to the front door and opened it ever so slightly. "Shoot! It's a cane burn," she groaned, referring to the antiquated method of igniting an entire crop of mature sugar cane to burn off the green foliage. "And dark clouds, too. Oh! No!"

She returned to bed and immediately fell asleep. Her phone rang an hour later. "Hi, Dawn. Looks like this drizzle is keeping me home this morning. Are you still joining me at the spa tomorrow?"

"I'm planning on it, sweetheart, but I need to inform you of something in case you want to cancel."

"What's wrong?"

"Karina, it's about Sky. There's a rumor going around that he stole a few things from Rosie."

"These rumors! I don't know what to think. I just heard it from someone else and it sounded so contrived. Did you hear any details?"

"There seldom are with rumors. I'm still calling clients regarding the ridiculous rumors about my corporation being in a financial mess. It's taken me weeks of phone calls to straighten out *that* mess and still there's no end in sight."

"I'm sorry."

"Well let's not think about my problems now. The rumors regarding Sky are most likely untrue; he's probably an innocent victim. If you haven't had any problems with him, then you shouldn't worry too much. Just give it a little thought."

"I can't help but think about it, but I'm not going to let it ruin my day. Are we still meeting tomorrow at one?"

"Absolutely, Ms. Karina. I'm planning on four hours of coddled debauchery. After the treatment I want to arrange a Mediterranean evening for you and it's absolutely my treat."

"The Med, huh. I'll wear my Gucci sandals. Thanks for being there and being my best friend. Ciao."

"Ciao. Sorry, sweetie, about these nasty rumors."

Karina felt like her world was crashing around her. Her entire world, her future hopes, everything was suddenly shaken. Were the rumors true? If not, why was this happening to her lover, her pal, and her confidant? Why was it happening to her?

She added a crepe lunch to her sybaritic schedule, hoping the chocolate and strawberry-mousse crepe would brighten her day. Still dejected after she ordered, she turned to the first page of her paperback.

After lunch, she went to Safeway for a week's worth of edibles. She had a premonition that she would run into Sky (possibly hanging around the melon section for some perverted reason). By the third aisle, her intuition of running into him was even stronger, and she couldn't get Dawn's comments out of her thoughts. She turned into the fourth aisle.

At the opposite end of aisle four, Rosie was pulling a Cheez Whiz from the shelf and looking at her. It was like a scene from *High Noon* as they both drew their carts up closer to their bodies. Karina slowly lowered a box of poppy and sesame crackers into her cart, while Rosie did the same with her can of "Cheezin 'n' Squeezin" Whiz. Sky's past and present girlfriends stared at each other down the long food corridor.

After they dropped their goods into the carts, both women rose to full height and stiffened. Neither woman ducked for cover, nor retreated toward the popcorn and nuts aisle. Poker-faced, they both dropped their arms; gunslinger and marshal on the dusty main street — resurrected.

The two shoppers simultaneously drew their wrists upward and clamped onto the cold metal handles of the shopping carts. They pushed forward. Their eye contact was steadfast, until they met — cart to cart. Rosie was standing beside the Honey Glazed Jerky display.

"Hi, I'm Rosie. We met at the Upcountry Thing recently."

"Yes, I remember. I'm Karina," she said nervously. They ignored their involvement in the pygmy-whale rescue.

"I'd love to chitchat, but there's one thing you should know — along with every other woman on this island. Sky hurt me *physically* when we were together. I should have gotten out of there earlier, but he kept taking me by surprise. Every woman around here should be warned! Sorry. Best of luck, but be careful and don't mention you heard anything from me, or he might get violent again. Sorry again. I really have to go."

"Oh, my God!" exclaimed Karina. "I already heard reports of his womanizing, and thought they were just rumors."

"No! No! That's true! And he stole some things from me, but I can't prove it. I'd better go, I've said too much."

"Thanks for telling me."

"Just watch out," warned Rosie as she swung her cart around and left.

Karina felt wounded and off balance. Her world of joy and security was yanked away, replaced by doubt and vulnerability. Her legs had gone weak; the cart kept her from collapsing. Could all these accusations be true?

She slowly pushed off. Sheer willpower moved her legs down the aisle, one small step at a time. Near the end, she regained control over her body and darted toward the door, leaving her cart behind.

How could she ignore all these warning bells? By the time she reached the exit she had her phone out and had punched Sky's number. He picked up on the third ring.

"Sky, I need to break this off! I keep hearing

about your troublesome past. *Now* I'm hearing about physical abuse! It's too scary. Sweetie, don't argue, *please!*"

"Don't you see what's happened? People believe her lies. I *never* hurt her. There's evil out there I can't fight. Please! Honey, I love you and would never hurt you in any way."

"I love you too, but I need to take a break and sort things out. Goodbye, Sky."

WILD BOAR

The mountain hunt for wild boar was set for tomorrow. Sky had mixed feelings about going, but Buddy had been prodding him for years. At the moment, he was standing on his special beach facing the ocean. Although there were plenty of rocks and stones scattered over his beach, he called it "Soothing Sands."

He didn't come here often, because of the pain associated with it — emotional pain that came with searching for answers to personal problems. There was another pain — at the tip of his elbow — as he stood throwing stones far into the ocean.

Karina had ended the relationship. She had ended the romance that held far more promise of passion, excitement, and longevity than any he had known before. And he was feeling anger, depression, and helplessness, all mixed together and each taking its turn.

I can't prove my innocence, he thought, as he threw a large beach pebble far beyond the surf line. He guessed that it flew over one hundred yards, which explained why his elbow stung again. He wondered if the sting was his measurement of emotional pain. At the moment he didn't care. Maybe surgery would be needed, but he intended to keep throwing these beach stones far into the ocean.

Sky looked down the beach. Not far away was the hill where, on more than one occasion, he had poured champagne into Karina's glass on top of that grassy knoll. Together, they had waited for the sunset flash of green and the pink afterglow of twilight. He was not going to let himself cry. Maybe he should call her? The same question begged an answer during every waking hour since the breakup.

He knew he had never loved anyone as much as he loved Karina. She made him come alive and rise above his reticent nature. Instinct told him to give her time, but instinct was torturing him at the moment — and allowing the relationship to wither away. He looked again to the ocean.

Sky thought about her compassion, her wit, and her child-like enthusiasm. She had the natural spirit of aloha — someone who belonged on Maui. He was surprised at how easy it was to trust everything about her. He sensed that she held a secret or two, but felt that if it affected their relationship she would reveal it in due time.

He looked down the coast at a distant beach. One of their favorite snorkel spots glistened in the morning sun. "Damn, she's everywhere," he mumbled. It was too much to think about. He chucked another stone as far as he could throw it. "God, that hurt." He was *not* going to cry.

Early the next morning, Sky had his head at the open window of Buddy's truck, to keep from getting sick on the jarring road. As a result of sucking dusty air, his blackened, gritty face qualified him for the brotherhood of coalminers. He listened to the hunting dogs in the back, yelping with excited anticipation.

"Hell, I think the boars have already won!" yelled Shafer, hanging onto the frame of the wind vent. "Between my wrenched back and choked lungs, I'm ready to check into Maui Memorial Medical Center."

"Hang on, brah," Buddy Kanoa yelled back. "I gonna find da lower gear or fo' sure we goin' backwards! We neva even reach da fun part; crawlin' on our knees in da boonies when no mo' trail."

Rattling up the curvy dirt road, the old Toyota was a bit of a rust bucket from years of catching salty air. The ravenous sea salt had devoured a fair portion of metal on the battered body of the truck, leaving some major holes and plenty of pockmarked craters. The paint job was a fading memory. There was concern that the passenger door would pull away from the last thread of rust, never to be attached again.

Bumpy, rutted, and nearly straight up in some stretches, the road was the only land access in the direction of the 5000-foot primeval peaks of the West Maui Mountains. A pineapple corporation owned the land and would haul in a grader about the time a rugged four-wheel drive declined the vertical challenge. On this first Saturday in June, "grader time" was overdue.

Buddy kept the pedal floored, worried that his gutless pickup truck would slow to a stall on the steep stretch and threaten to roll back. The faded green ti leaf, tied under the bottom of his back bumper, hung down like a mare's tail. It was dried out and spindly, and there was concern that the good luck symbol had lost its protective powers.

It had been almost an hour of bouncing along a rocky track since they left the Lahaina Pali Highway, and the adventure pals, along with their four hunting dogs, were still some distance from the west-slope trailhead. Wild pig hunting was their aim for the morning. Buddy had a permanent boar hunting permit from the state, allowing him to blast away anytime at the destructive feral animals. It was Sky's first venture into mountainous pig hunting.

"I'm ready for anything that gets rounded up for us, but I'd be content to take back an old axis deer or an ornery ram," kidded Sky. "I know you need kalua pork for your lu'au next month, but venison stew or a 'billy burger' would satisfy my appetite."

"We see what da pups round up."

The feral pigs in this area were, without a doubt, the most ferocious mammals on Maui and were cursed with faces not even their mothers could love. Unfortunately for the beauty-challenged beasts, they favored the taste of vanishing native Hawaiian plants — behavior not endorsed by the park service.

The horned-pig species, foolishly imported from Europe, had penetrated the mountain slopes. The ill-tempered marauders were particularly adept at annihilating fragile native flora. They eroded the soil searching for earthworms, fed on the fleshy core of tree-fern trunks and endemic plants, and created mud wallows, harboring lethal mosquito breeding pools.

"We make it so far," growled Buddy, stopping the truck. "Can take one short break and wash down dis damn dust wit' couple Buds." He popped off the cover of the water container, which was strapped into a corner of the truck bed. The dogs were ready for refreshment and a chance to stretch their legs.

"The dogs are excited," said Sky, as he watched them circle the clearing.

"Yeah, dis pack one good one. Couple of da pups are ole pals of mine and dey knows dea business, fo' real."

Above them, a thick mist drifted across the peaks, shrouding and caressing each crest, like a manta ray gliding over a forest of soft coral. A lighter mist surrounded the tailgate, which had been converted to a beer bench. Ten pounds of ice kept the supply of beer chilled in the cooler.

Across the central valley, they could see the smooth sloping crown of Haleakala. Otherwise known as the "House of the Sun," it dominated the clear view to the east. The east Maui mountain evoked Hawaiian mythical and spiritual deference.

"If I get dis baby to start one mo' time, maybe she can remember her low gears. If she no can, we goin' take one helluva hike."

"I don't mind," said Sky. "To tell you the truth, I'm worried more about the brakes on this rusty relic for our downhill plummet."

"Who said got brakes? We jus' stick it in low, and let dem embankments slow us down." Sky's face turned to shock. "Heh, jus' kiddin'," Buddy said, laughing. "No worry, da brakes is good."

"That's a comfort," said Sky. "I was already thinking that it's a good day for a stroll down a mountain."

"We betta get out da short ponchos," Buddy suggested. "Dis rainforest no see sun fer long. One year dey measure 50 feet rain up at Pu'u Kukui peak. Dat's not countin' ten mo' from da 'fog drip.' Musta got a team of divers fer take da readings.

"Sorry to hear 'bout you and Karina. Hope you no mind my talk 'bout it. She one classy lady. You guys da original peas in da pod."

"Thanks, Buddy. Let's not talk about it now. It's too painful, and I figured today would be a good opportunity to get away from the whole thing. So, how did it go with that purple lady we saw you with at the upcountry shindig?" Sky washed down the road powder from his grimy throat with quick gulps of beer.

"Brah, maybe you no believe it. Under dat purple wig live one of da sweetest sistas I meet in long time. She only part-time at da Lavender Store. Dat outfit has one big lavender farm upcountry. Joni's da one dat puts on teas for da tourists. They sit around da porch and suck up tea and lavender lemonade. Spose to take out stress and give da sex drive mo' juice."

"I remember the farms from my travels in England; the garden teas were a popular attraction. I can't believe 'Captain Charm' needs any of that medicinal magic, especially with your libido. So did you try the benefits on Joni?"

"You know my monk rule fer first month, Sky guy. Maybe I be one animal, but first da gentleman. Best part is she loves da water, and she even one scuba diver."

"She sounds perfect. A lot more going for her than a large pair of, uhhh... lavender lips."

"Yeah," Buddy replied, wincing at the jest. "Next weekend we goin' divin'. Maybe see whitetip sharks in da caves at Makena Landing. She one funny lady. Da whole time somethin' 'bout her make me laugh. By da way, hear you and Rosie take one small powwow dat mornin' at da winery."

"Talk about sweet. That little social muffin puts out the sweetest aloha on this island. Rosie was all smiles and friendly chatter last weekend. In fact, Karina started to bond with her. I had to mention that underneath that sociable exterior lurks a revengeful nut case.

"Her friend, lanky Liz, came dressed as a beaded buckarette. Too bad she doesn't suit your plebian tastes, big guy, because she's loaded with plantation houses. All you need to do is bring her some lavender lemonade and massage her skinny neck on the veranda."

"Joni's plenty much woman for me. Dem two wahine make good pair, tall Liz and your little ex-cupcake. Sorry brah, jus' kiddin'. Maybe you still sensitive, but hey, long time ago dat breakup."

"Seriously, old pal, I need your advice," said Sky. "You seem to have pretty good luck with women. How come you never get trashed by any ex-girlfriends? Were they all wonderfully sane and genuinely grateful for the wild 'Buddy ride'? What's your secret?"

"Jus' one t'ing, but you gotta keep 'tween me and you."

"OK, Mr. Kanoa, I promise."

"Now dis is jus' 'tween us. When I wit' one of dem lovely ladies, I mention I like keep privacy. I say no lady talk stink 'bout me. Meanwhile, my 'decoy' jus' waitin' in back a da carport slider. It's a small freezer wit' one wide piece of duck tape stretched across da door. Only need use it one time."

"What the heck for?"

"One day t'ings change wit' dis lady, and she like talk 'bout what she gonna do if we broke up. I left da slider open the next day. Dat night she spot it, and we stand for while, listenin' to da motor hummin', 'fore she ask 'bout it. I said it from da past and no like talk 'bout it. The sight of dat duct tape gives me 'chicken skin' already, so don't know what t'inking she doin'.

"It's jus' for emergency, but da damn t'ing work good dat night. I never hear nothin' but sweet from her after dat. Later, we had us one friendly breakup."

"Wow! I promise not to mention it."

"Aw, it's empty 'cept a baking soda. Man, I wish you good luck with all dat phony gossip. Nothin' worse den an angry ole hound nippin' at your ass."

"Yeah, and if things get any worse I might just stick that freezer outside a certain Ma'alaea condo."

"No worry now. Let's slug down dis Bud and fire up da Japanese clunker. Maybe she ready try 4-wheel action."

Somewhere overhead, a wayward crested honeycreeper cried out, singing a song of survival. Buddy thought the loud defiant cry was a good omen for their mission; he turned his attention toward the dogs. "Whoa, Scout! Now!" he bellowed, breaking the silence of the thick air. The dogs loped back to the truck.

They drove through a wispy cloudbank and parked; the last stretch of ruts was washed out. The four hunting dogs hit the ground running, with Scout in the lead and Makawao right behind his rump. Choke and Old Pecos were circling the clearing.

Pecos had seen his share of hunts over his 15 feisty years, and had lost a step or two, but he was often the first one to sail through the air and land on the prey. He wasn't particular either about the size of the enemy, and tackled 500-pound boars with the same intensity as a mongoose. Clever hunting skills kept him alive. Buddy gave one shrill whistle blast and Scout trotted back to the truck with his yipping pals in tow.

"Brah, now we need brush off any alien seeds from da boots 'fore we get to da fragile zone. Stud fella like you probably packin' plenty spunky seeds."

"Hey, big guy, at least my clothes have seen some laundry work in the last month, unlike *your* seasoned hunting ensemble."

Buddy wanted Sky to experience the hunt in the traditional "Portuguese style" favored by a few of the old timers, but seldom used anymore. There would be no guns for protection. Both men carried pig stickers inside open-ended sheaths on their army belts. The blade on Sky's pig knife measured ten inches.

Today, Sky had the "guest honor" of stabbing the feral intruder if everything went according to plan. Buddy carried a slightly smaller version, capable of many tasks. He also carried a sizable first aid kit in his backpack, equipped with large sewing needles. A machete was strapped to his pack for jungle-slashing access.

"If it's a ole tusker, hope you get to dem pups in time." My two 'grabbers' sure as hell appreciate it. OK, Scout! Here's da way. Got it. Now go!" The command to the poi dog roared into the wet cloudbank.

They followed the dogs higher into the mountain. Both wore camouflage shirts and water-proof hiking boots. Sky wore his oldest, most beat-up safari hat. After two hours, even Buddy wasn't sure of their location and kept checking his compass. Suddenly the dogs were yelping; the noise was just below them. This time the yelps were close together and loud.

"Let's go!" Buddy yelled. "Dey sound serious." They took turns crashing and burrowing through the thick plants with moves a Packers fullback would have applauded. In spite of his limp, Sky was juking and charging as fast as the terrain allowed. By the time they approached the dogs, they were both ripped and bleeding.

The pack was already biting at the boar when they reached the tiny clearing. When the dogs heard their master approach, they leaped onto the big tusker. The sounds of the barking dogs and the squealing of the pig were deafening.

Choke had a death grip on the boar's ear. Pecos had a marginal grip on the side of its neck. Scout was trying unsuccessfully to secure the tail, and Makawao was circling around the chaotic noise acting as cheerleader.

Buddy entered the clearing first and quickly decided that there might be time for Sky to run up and give the plunge. The 120-pound boar thrashed his head back and forth in the hope of ripping canine flesh. By the time Sky reached the chaos, the noise level was incredible, and his heart was pumping from the sprint through the underbrush.

"Poke em, poke em, poke em!" Buddy yelled above the roar. Sky buried his knife into the pig's chest. He stabbed again. "Twist! Twist! No pull! Twist!" Buddy shouted. His words finally connected and Sky gave a twist in the boar's chest near the heart. The squealing stopped, but the dogs were still crazed.

"Settle down," roared Buddy, as he plucked the three pit bull mongrels from their gripping and chomping before they damaged the fast-dying pig.

"Damn, I can't believe how hot this gushing blood is!" Sky gasped, clearly shaken, but in a strange way exhilarated by the moment. His entire arm was soaked in blood — and not all of it was from the prize catch.

"It's hot cause dat mean buggah running fo' his damn life," said Buddy, sounding overly macho considering the fuzzy feeling of pride he felt for his hunting pal. "Congratulations, ole pal. Now we skin it and gut it. Den we cut it in half and bag it in da gunnies. We need bury da guts real deep. Old Pecos earned da big prize today — da heart."

The dogs were covered with pig splatter, thickened with mud and blood. They would stink to hog heaven until they returned home to face the jet spray from the water hose.

"These dogs are amazing." said Sky, gathering his breath and finally feeling his thumping heart soften a little. "I'm blown away."

"Yeah, I like t'ink dey all mine and not borrowed from da other guys. Dis pack be always changin'. Da mutts get killed, and sometimes demoted fo' bad performance, but Scout and Old Pecos been 'roun' long time."

After preparing the pig, they headed back; but soon they heard excited yipping somewhere down the hill.

"Go!" yelled Buddy, but Sky was already sprinting ahead, dropping his cumbersome pack along the way.

Below them a wide clump of false staghorn ferns, lantana, and blackberry vines with no earthly foundation, cantilevered more than ten feet beyond the cliff's edge. The mesh of terrestrial ferns, tough berry vines, and moisture-loving forest vegetation completely camouflaged a 20-foot steep and rocky drop-off.

Scout was at the bottom barking in panic after he plummeted down the hill. Makawao raced across the ferns toward the frenzied barking of his fallen comrade — unaware of the danger. After a long free-fall, Makawao landed headfirst on a sharp rock. Old

Pecos and Choke were right behind, although they slipped through a different pitfall in the overhang and didn't tumble as far down the slope.

Sky was right behind them. Suddenly, he had the sensation of a trapdoor opening and only gravity beneath. Finally he hit the slope and rolled. He tried to brace himself as he somersaulted to the bottom. "Stop! Stop! Stop!" he yelled at Buddy.

He screamed in spite of grinding through the dirt and tumbling through the hillside ground cover. He rolled to a halt just before crashing into a large volcanic rock. "It's a cliff! Stop!" He was bruised, but nothing was broken. He looked over and knew that Makawao was dead.

Although the direction of the yelping dogs was elusive in the thick forest, Buddy could tell Sky's position after his first warning shout. He stopped a few feet before the "fern ambush," and took a step back from the overgrown cliff. He found another route down and joined the survivors.

"Sorry about your tracker dog, Buddy."

"Yeah," he answered with a lump in his throat. "Makawao no mo'. I goin' miss em plenty. He had one good spirit." Buddy paused, started to speak, and then paused again. Sky looked away. Buddy cleared his throat, but his voice cracked when he spoke again. "He neva once... get da heart. We give em one good grave and den we go home. You gonna be OK?"

"Yeah," Sky replied. He already knew this would be his first and last hunt.

SPA AT THE GRAND

3:13. Large red numbers glared from the alarm clock. Karina's mind raced between thoughts of Sky and her teenage marriage. She couldn't slow her thoughts down, let alone switch gears and think about something else. And she couldn't slow that damn clock down, ticking her life away. She wondered if her romance with Sky had been too good to be true.

There had been only a few minutes of troubled sleep all night. She glared back at the clock, knowing that it was better to keep her eyes open. Otherwise, she was not only looking into Sky's face, but she was feeling his strong body against her own.

She felt a sense of déjà vu. At the innocent age of nineteen she had married the most exciting man she could imagine. Everything was perfect, and the future held nothing but promise. Together, they dreamed of one day living on a tropical island.

He was a smart, handsome Norwegian and her high school sweetheart. She fell madly in love with him — until the night he announced he was gay. He had been equally shocked at the discovery and as kind and apologetic to her as he could be. She left him the next day. Three weeks later she flew to

America, but continued to care about him and keep in contact.

There would be other men in her life, but never with the possibility of marriage — until now. They were merely flings, and she hadn't felt an intense passion or a reason for commitment —until now.

She thought about how her husband's announcement came without warning. For weeks now, she had been hearing warning bells about Sky. She silently chastised herself. Why did I allow myself to fall so head over heels for him?

When she finally decided to end it, she thought it would be quick and easy, and now she realized that there would be nothing easy about it. She was beating herself up. "Stop it!" she groaned.

Karina loved everything about Sky. He made her feel like a queen and was the most generous man that she had ever encountered. More importantly, she was sure he was in love with her. The red numbers read **5:23,** and a hint of morning light snuck around the curtain when Karina mumbled the word "angel," before falling asleep.

By the time Dawn Paris arrived at the "Grand" later that afternoon, Karina had chosen her spa program, the Metabolic Booster. She loved the tantalizing sounds of the ingredients: Terme Hydrotherapy, followed by an Exfoliating Crushed Grape Seed Scrub, and this followed by a Zen Trilogy Body Masque.

The cleansing trio groomed her for a 60-minute massage with Kukui Essential Oils. She always chose a manicure for a decompressing wrap-up. She sighed just thinking how relaxing it would be.

When Dawn entered the spa lobby, Karina was sipping a glass of water.

"It's lemon-cucumber. Want some? The cucumber taste is really refreshing."

"Hello, Karina. I'll have a glass, and I'll spare you my favorite cucumber rejoinder."

"Thanks Dawn, it hasn't been that long anyway. I love your hair. New color? You look like you lost a few pounds too."

"It's called champagne. It works for me, but my latest diet has been disappointing. There's 15 miserable pounds to go. I'm hoping you were blessed with some sleep last night. Are you really Sky-less?"

"Yeah, damn it! After our programs, we need to talk. I tossed all night, but finally got a few winks this morning. Are you really taking me to the Mediterranean this evening? You know I love surprises."

"Sweetheart, think Italian with some international touches along the way. Now which manner of debauchery have you chosen for your afternoon program?"

"I'm sticking with my favorite. The Lomi Lomi lava-stone massage claims to reach the deepest kinks. I don't know if it can reach the heart, but it's worth a try. Let's go, they're waving us in."

The lava stones produced warm avocado-scented sensations that permeated Karina's entire body. The soothing treatment warded off any chance of bitterness, at least for the moment. The facial, the foot reflexology, and the scalp massage were harmoniously therapeutic. She chose the Honey Steam Wrap for her finale. Any angry toxins that she carried into the salon were steamed away, leaving her in a relaxed state of confusion.

"Look, Dawn, there's Liz Brinkley getting a massage. Do you know her?"

"I know who she is, but I've never met her. It looks like she's getting a shiatsu from Rosie's friend, Kako Kaneshiro — everyone calls her Gecko. Yesterday, when I set up our appointments I requested massages from any therapist, but Ms. Kaneshiro. Hope it didn't sound too disparaging," Dawn added conspiratorially.

"Let's just smile and leave," said Karina. "I'm feeling too relaxed to chatter with any of Rosie's partners in crime. After I shower off these oils, I intend to slip into my gold Gucci's for the Italian tour. Later, sweetie. Ciao."

The ever-vigilant Elizabeth Brinkley had spotted them across the salon. This, in spite of lying on her back with her head dropped over the bench while her friend worked on her.

"Gecko, I can't believe that woman is still fooling around with Sky Shafer! She *must* have heard about all the hell that Rosie went through last year!"

"Sure, but it couldn't have been easy for Rosie to lose a stallion like that, Liz. In spite of the problems, Rosie talked about the hours of incredible sex. The stud service alone would have kept me in the fold."

Liz said, "I wonder if Sky's nervous about 'separation jinx,' knowing that every one of Rosie's former husbands died within two years of splitting up?"

"Maybe the jinx is broken, since they never married," said Gecko. "And then again, maybe he'll be number four. The timing of those three men is sure odd. I know her first husband had that heart defect, but the last two.... What do you think?"

"I'm not sure, but it's pretty damn bizarre the way the last two died. Fredrick driving his car under that sand truck and then getting buried alive when it flipped over. Roger's death was even spookier, falling out of a canoe late at night in the middle of the channel. It seems like a hell of a lot of bad luck follows Rosie's men. Maybe Sky should have a bodyguard."

"I wouldn't mind guarding his body and limbering up those artistic muscles. Hopefully he doesn't have a heart condition, because there would be no letting up from me."

"Gecko, it's time you got lucky, but right now it's time you concentrate on my left shoulder."

A loud thump greeted Karina and Dawn as they stepped outside the resort hotel into a world of elegant cascading pools and waterfalls, all flowing toward the beach. A hotel landscaper was high overhead, hoisted on a "Genie" hydraulic lift near the top of one of the four-story royal palms. He had sawed off a 50-pound seedpod from the towering tree. The pod, resembling a smooth skinny missile, landed with such force it created a small crater in the manicured lawn.

"Was that the signal for the start of our Riviera rendezvous?" asked Karina. "That's quite a phallic-looking weapon."

"Lucky for us the boys roped off the bombing range," said Dawn. "It's an ongoing struggle keeping the tourists from getting thumped by falling coconuts, palm seed husks, and branches. Think of that crater as someone's kneecap, relaxing under the shade of a palm tree."

The 40 silver-white, royal palms lining the pool were part of the Grand's original 30 million-dollar art budget.

"Sweetheart, this spot must be one of the most picturesque places on Maui," said Dawn.

"I've heard they cost $10,000 apiece."

"That's true, but they probably recovered that expense from their advertising images. The royals make a powerful, linear artistic statement framing the reflection pool. At the end of the pool you can see bronzed dolphins leaping toward those fountain jets. In a less grandiose way, it reminds me of the Taj Mahal reflection pool leading to the palace. Luckily, the dolphins and the colorful koi fish keep it tropical."

"The dolphins look like they're fanning out in front of a boat," said Karina. "They remind me of the dolphin escorts off Lana'i harbor. Let's see, a Taj pool surrounded by open-air Moroccan cabanas. I'd say your tour is off to a world-class start. What's next?"

They walked through a labyrinth of fountains, swimming pools, water slides, and blue and gold tiled spas. A breeze wafted plumeria and Coppertone scents across the water features.

"First we start with a mood enhancer at the Volcano Bar. Then you can show off your Gucci slippers at Ferraro's bar in the Four Seasons. Eventually we'll wind our way along the coastal garden walk to a Moorish-Spanish style villa with an Italian restaurant called Ciao. Think of it as an international escapade."

The Volcano Bar proved to be too noisy. After a pair of rum-based Lava Flows, they passed the restaurant, "Humuhumunukunukuapua'a," named after the colorful triggerfish. They paused to admire the Polynesian thatched roof eatery, located in the middle of a salt water lagoon. Various reef fish were in a feeding frenzy; the catered surface was so crowded that a few of the bright colored ocean-dwellers were leaping out of the water. A small group of humuhumu joined the fracas.

As the churning water settled, they continued

their outing and entered the stunning Wailea sea walk. The "hummer man" approached, loping along at his usual cocky pace.

"Check out the 'hummer man,' whispered Karina. "I think 'mafia' every time I see his face. He always has the same attire; a white, unbuttoned, dress shirt exposing that skimpy bikini. Oh, and the black 'Maui Jims' wrapped over his scarred cheeks.

"Look back, Dawn. He's way too tall a target to be a hit man, but that face has seen some violence. His humming melodies never seem to match his swaggering attitude. He's creepy, like the 'saunter of evil.'"

"I can see that he clearly stands out among these honeymooners and after-work joggers, but your misplaced mobster is probably just a sweet grandpa."

The late afternoon sun had lit the upper edges of a couple clouds hanging over the horizon. They selected a prime ocean view table at Ferraro's; a violinist was playing for the early-bird dinner crowd.

"Karina, here're my thoughts. I'll make them short and crisp so we can get on with our Mediterranean journey. You already know my history with Sky; two dates many years ago leading to zero romance. None of those cute little pheromones yanked us from our dinner tables and took us into the 'dance of love,' not to mention any chemistry cupids keeping us awake all night with animated conversation. But there's always been a lot of respect for each other, and we've maintained a solid friendship ever since."

Dawn paused briefly and then continued, "I don't know everything about Sky at the moment, and I understand that some people can change over time. Yes, the rumors are awful, but I've never once heard any accusations about him. Unless there's some kind of hard evidence, I think you should give him the benefit of the doubt."

"But...."

"No, please let me finish. Another thing I want to mention is the source of the rumors. Rosie has a bubbly personality and is respected in the community for her animal work and her popular causes. I know, because we're on a couple of committees together. But the fact that she was unusually bitter about her ex-husbands after they separated, and the fact that every husband died a couple of years later troubles me. Do you know how they died?"

"I know they were freaky, but accidental. I wasn't on island when they happened."

"You've got the freaky part right!" exclaimed Dawn. "Her second husband... oh, I've forgotten his name, turned the corner at the end of North Kihei Road at the same time a truck carrying beach sand approached from the opposite direction. The truck driver swore he never saw the car driving right at him until the last second. When the trucker swerved, his trailer flipped and dumped the entire load on the car. He was buried in sand and suffocated because the windows were open."

"How horrible! What could be worse luck than that?"

"I think the death of her third husband Roger was worse. He had been dating Rosie's friend, Betty, and they went out kayaking off the Lahaina pali coast late one afternoon. It was only his second time kayaking and maybe the first time for Betty. The offshore winds caught them by surprise right before dark, and the currents took them toward Kahoʻolawe. Betty said that he was acting a little crazy and

120

incoherent, and then they both fell asleep in their kayak sometime after midnight.

"When she awoke, he was gone and she was miles from Maui. A fishing boat found her the next afternoon, dehydrated and frightened out of her mind. His body was never found, but there're lots of sharks out there. Afterwards, there was some local speculation, but without a motive the talk died down."

"Dawn, I could have happily spent the rest of my years on Maui without hearing *those* stories. You may be right about Sky being the victim in all this. I have to wait a little longer before I call him, just to be sure. When I'm ready, can I ask you to pave the way for me?"

"Of course."

Turning once again onto the Wailea coastal walk, they kept glancing at the sun, which was preparing to take the plunge. The golden fireball fashioned a shiny silver lining along the entire length of the ocean horizon before departing. The sky was filled with brushstrokes of only one color — ruby red. A brilliant half-moon witnessed the earth's rosiness from high above.

On the mauka side of the path, an overhead forest of beach naupaka plants loaded with little white flowers, encroached onto the narrow walkway. Giant red spider lilies fought for breathing space between the naupakas.

"What the heck was that!" exclaimed Karina, ducking toward the cliff edge as something whizzed over her head.

"Wedge-tailed shearwaters. They come for a month to nest in these steep Wailea Point cliffs. Normally they swoop in from the sea, not over the path."

"Another one! It's like they're strafing us, but

we can't see their swoops in the dark until the last second," Karina said, enthralled. "Those large wings are dramatic and the light catching their white bellies... wow! And I thought that goofy cattle egret doing the hula on the lawn with its stringy neck was the show for today."

"Unfortunately, the feral cats have been finding most of the shearwater nests. It's a shame because they have this mystical, almost monotone haunting cry at night. Seems somewhat spiritual to me, but you can't always hear them because of the surf. The problem is we have thousands of feral cats. About the same number as realtors," Dawn joked, changing her tone.

"Yeah, besides us and a few other folks, it's all realtors and massage therapists," Karina added playfully.

They strolled around the lava rock inlets, listening to the waves lap the underbelly of hollowed-out caves. The coastal trail sloped down to another picturesque beach. They timed their grand entrance perfectly; the renowned resort before them was handsomely illuminated.

Karina squealed with the joy of a wide-eyed child. "I have never seen the Kea Lani at this time of day, nor from this direction. Look! The turret is lit up! It looks like a swirled vanilla softy-cone. The tiki torches around the pools are magic. With the architecture and the night lighting, we could be in Morocco, or Spain, or somewhere along the Med. It's so foreign for Maui."

"Some would say a touch too Disneyfied. It's similar to the Las Hadas in Mexico and has some features inspired from the Alhambra fortress in Granada, Spain. I hope you'll like my dinner spot,

Café Ciao. Maybe we'll get a dark furry-armed waiter with an Italian tongue."

"Dawn, I love all your choices today. I'm grateful to have such a supportive friend. Let's reminisce over dinner about last summer's trip to Europe."

After pasta and red wine, they headed back along the cliff. Dawn had forgotten that the narrow coastal walk was unlit. It wandered through overgrown walls of thick bushes. Unfortunately, the beacon from the half-moon was hidden behind clouds.

"Sorry, I forgot a flashlight," said Dawn. "It's almost impossible to see the path. Try and stay away from the cliff.

"Karina, listen! Did you hear that? Those moaning sounds aren't 'night marchers.' They're shearwaters taking roll call in the cliffs. As more of the group identify themselves, that ethereal monotone changes to a gentle melody."

"They sound ghostly! But what the heck are night marchers?"

"Ghosts. I'm sorry I brought that up. Another time might be more appropriate to tell you ghost stories about the Hawaiian battlefield warriors."

"Thanks for *that*! I was already imagining the hummer man prowling behind us. If you wanted to add more excitement to your therapeutic tour, you succeeded."

CARNAL CROONERS

The Vixens gathered at the palatial Makena home of Ms. Elizabeth R. Brinkley. They had a couple of things on their mind, but the fabulous food, creatively catered by Giorgio's, was on the back burner. The scent of young men lit up the front burners.

"I like the ambience," said Rosie. "Low lights, spicy food, young hunks, and games to keep it casual."

"Yeah, Liz, I didn't know you had this big party-room," said Gecko excitedly. "Can I challenge the guys to a game of pool?"

"Of course. There aren't any rules here, except swimsuits aren't allowed in the indoor swimming pool and spa area. Pace yourself because the young gentlemen will be here until dawn. They're close friends of some of my younger friends so there's no worry tonight.

"I suggest we start building our strength with oysters on the half-shell, and empower our libidos with eel and octopus sashimi. There will be tons of food all night long, but now I want you to meet these yummy guys at the billiard table.

"As you know gentlemen, tonight we are having

a theme party. Everyone here is a singer from the sixties. The idea is to have fun, so let's all get into it.

"Now *please* meet the raspy-throated fireball with the raven hair, Ms. Janis J. And — *please* welcome this dynamic bundle of raw energy, direct from Tokyo, the curvaceous and robust Tina T. As you can see I am the statuesque Cherokee — Cher.

"Divas, this *is* the 'Whole Lotta Shakin' all-night long, Mr. Jerry Lee L. And here we have another raspy-throated singer — say hello to the ambidextrous Rod S.

"And *finally* we have on this stage tonight the answer to whether he is, and wherever he is — *please* meet Elvis." Gecko giggled so loud that she could barely say hello. Rosie had the biggest smile the Vixens had ever seen.

"Now that all you crooners have something in common, we can adjourn to the lounge area for some spicy pupu. We have the servers from Giorgio's for the next hour, so relax and allow your taste buds to be fired up. There's karaoke music after dinner, featuring *your* greatest hits. Each of you has to sing at least one song, so let the champagne loosen those lips and clear the cobwebs from your vocal cords."

Liz suffered from compulsive quantity overkill when ordering cuisine. The tables at her societal affairs seemed to accumulate half of the island's food supply. The Giorgio servers knew in advance to bring plenty of take-home bags.

After sampling the abundant pupu, the Vixens gathered in the kitchen while the young crooners picked up billiard cues. It was time for the ladies to digest the appetizers and reflect on the upcoming dessert, which involved igniting a different group of secretion glands.

"The men are as excited as you are," announced Liz. "They may be in their mid-twenties, but they're feeling like kids in a candy store. Don't go getting any urges to be matronly. You can get as silly as you want with them.

"In addition, they're all hard-bodied surfers familiar with riding waves all day; it's unlikely you'll cause them to wipe-out."

"Well, I *definitely* like playful," said Rosie. "In the past, my relationships always started out playful, but then... I don't know, something changed and they became boring."

"Mine were always silly, but none of them lasted long," admitted Gecko.

"My relationships have always been costly," griped Liz. "That's why it's easier for me to pay for short-term affairs and not sign the big contract with 'Mr. Perfect.'"

"Lucky you, for being able to financially swing it," said Rosie.

"Good for you, Cher," said Gecko. "I would do the same thing if I had the means. I'm always trying too hard to please guys."

"I think it's OK to please your mate," said Rosie, "but if your mate changes his behavior in a relationship, then I think all previous commitments get thrown out the window. There must be accountability. Otherwise, we have a right to insure that justice gets done."

"I think we would both agree with that, Janis," said Liz. "Now let's mingle with the 'vocalists' before they switch to a game of pocket pool. Anyone have a first pick?"

"Thanks for asking. I think I'll go find out where Elvis has been hiding all these years," joked Rosie.

"I'm ready for a 'Whole Lotta Shakin,'" declared Gecko, blushing at the notion that her rambunctious libido was about to be addressed.

Later, Elvis sang his heart out for Rosie, so to speak, but she felt they didn't harmonize, or maybe she uncovered him in his waning years. A short time later, she discovered Rod S. swimming naked in the heated pool.

"Hopefully you're saving a couple of laps for me," she flirted.

Rod stood up in the shallow end and flipped his hair so expertly that most of the water flew off. The singer's fine-tuned instrument was buoyant in the clear water.

"No clothes allowed here, Ms. Janis J.," he bellowed, so that his voice would rumble across the pool. Then he gave her a wide smile; it was easy to interpret his inviting eyes. "May I help you disrobe?"

"I'm quite capable of disrobing Mr. Rod — I mean Mr.... well now! Rod seems to be an appropriate name for you." Rosie was enchanted by his grin, as well as, flustered at the sight of him.

"Slip in, it's warm and I give the best head massage on the island."

"Oh boy. Where were you 20 years ago?" She dropped her robe and sat down on the middle step, feeling the exceptionally warm water around her. She lowered her feet into the shallow end, exposing the rest of her body to the steamy indoor air. Rod slowly glided over to the trio of steps and dawdled in front of her as if they had all night long.

"I'm glad you found me," said Rod.

"Likewise."

The small talk was brief and Rod was as good as his word. Janis J. closed her eyes and tried to remember the words to her hit song *Down On Me*. She hummed softly.

"That was really nice," she panted, "I've never known it quite like... oh, never mind."

"My pleasure, J.J.. Would you like to go in the back for a complete massage?"

"I'd like that. Let me take a lap across the pool first and then you can take me to your lair. OK to ask some questions along the way?"

"Sure. In a way I feel like I already know you, maybe from an earlier life."

"Seriously, Rod, I feel the same."

As the evening turned the corner and midnight announced a new day, Rosie became even more mesmerized with Rod. Intimate conversation replaced their sporadic lusts. Rosie felt strangely connected to Rod, and expressed feelings never before shared. Maybe it was his effeminate nature, or maybe it was the flowing of white wine, but she felt free to speak her mind. Besides, she would never see this young man again; he didn't even know her name.

"So you've never had, let's say, aggressive sex?" Rod asked.

"No, never! Sex was always great without roughing it up. But I will say that the jerk in my last relationship made me become physically aggressive."

Rosie's voice started to slur; her expression became glazed. "I was always suspicious of the amount of time he spent away from me. I even followed him a few times, but he was too clever. He was seeing someone else, though, and we got into fights over that! He forced me to become violent, and I clobbered him a few times.

"After we separated, I became even angrier. The idea that he dumped me! Later, I told my friends that *he* physically abused *me*. Don't you think we have a right to teach people a lesson?"

"Not really, but it sounds different for you. I know some guys can be jerks, also some women I've met."

"Maybe I should have forgotten those guys, but I can't seem to move on unless all accounts are ... Anyway, thanks for listening."

"No problem. How about a foot massage?"

"Yeah," she said exhaustedly, "and maybe a nap."

It was late morning when the Vixens gathered at the breakfast table for pastries and coffee. The young singing trio had left soon after dawn; there was a favorable south-shore swell for surfing. Gecko was bubbly, but Rosie and Liz looked drained.

"It's the first time I missed church in a while," said Rosie, "but I had a pretty good reason. We don't have a confessional, so your sanctuary turned out to be positively divine."

"I'll say!" exclaimed Gecko, "I feel like a born-again fox. Mr. Jerry Lee was non-stop."

"Surprisingly, Elvis and I discovered we sang the same tune," said Liz. "I had a good time with him, which was fortunate for me, since I never saw Rod or Jerry Lee again after you guys latched on."

"Thanks, Cher," said Rosie, "I need to head home."

"Yeah, thanks, Cher," said Gecko, "I'm going too, but maybe I'll stop off at a couple of surfing sites along the way."

SEETHING STUDIO

Sky held his ultra-fine brush over the painting. He concentrated on the area below the gill, and then added an orange fleck to the small crescent beauty mark on the humuhumu-fish. The precise dab took a steady hand as the giclee canvas print, reproduced by a high-quality ink jet, needed a bright color to make it "near-original."

Sky Shafer's paintings had been described as "whimsical sea harmony." It was one of many descriptions given to his artwork, although it may have captured it best. His talents led him, from time to time, toward other artistic ventures, such as bronze sculptures of sea creatures. But he always returned to his first love, marine-life oil paintings.

Sixteen years ago he experimented with a somewhat fanciful style, featuring a frolicking sea-life community both above and below the ocean's reefs. The style became known as "dual worlds." The underwater foreground of his paintings depicted brightly illustrated sea characters with joyful expressions, representing the motion and interaction of life below the sea. The sharp cliffs, jagged mountains, and pristine beaches painted in the background were no less dramatic, representing the serene harmonic nature found on a beautiful island.

He hovered over the large, oblong table, strategically positioned in the center of the room. He believed that energy from the churning ocean rose through the battered old floorboards and ascended to his work-in-progress. At high tide he could hear the surf slosh across the old timber and concrete pilings and slap at the whaling-era planks underneath.

Sky was convinced the creativity that metamorphosed into brush strokes emanated from the frothing sea below. The room rumbled with noise and movement from the surging shore water. Collectors often told him that they could smell the ocean in his paintings. He understood why.

His studio was in the rickety rear section of the building that housed his showy Lahaina Front Street gallery.

The intercom buzzed unexpectedly. "Mr. Sky, this is Boomer in the gallery. Dawn Paris is here. She's very adamant about seeing you. Can I bring her in?"

"Of course. She's an old friend."

Boomer, his trusted top salesman and spelunking buddy, led Dawn past the center island of waterfalls and floor-to-ceiling aquariums, straight to the rear wall of the gallery. He discreetly touched a switch under a sales desk and part of the back wall opened slightly. A short, secret hallway led directly to Sky's studio. Inside the studio, the wiry redhead gave a conspiratorial wink to Sky and turned back, closing the door behind Dawn.

The outside walls of the studio harbored giant portholes with floor-mounted telescopes. One pointed at the busy harbor mouth; another aimed at the mob of tourists on Front Street.

"How's my old buddy?" asked Sky, giving his friend and former date-mate a welcome kiss and warm hug.

"Hello, Sky. I see you're as prolific as ever, and I must say that your colors are still the most vibrant around the islands. Is that a new edition you're working on?"

"Somewhat new. It's a giclee reproduction I'm touching up. If you're looking for an original, I can give you a 60 percent 'special friend' discount — say fifty-thousand cash. It would just about cover my monthly rent."

"Very funny, you know my budget. I think you also know the reason I'm here."

"I'm hoping there's good news. Care for a cabernet?"

"Sure. Apparently happy hour starts earlier in this tourist town, so why not? The reason I'm here is because of a precious person whom we both know and love. Karina's been absolutely miserable without you for the last month, and you should know that part of her fear comes from an experience from a previous relationship. Something traumatic. I'm not sure exactly what happened, but I think it was a long time ago. Right now, well... she's just determined to be extra cautious."

"You know I happen to believe that trust is the most important component in a relationship," said Sky. "Since the day she called and broke things off, I knew she was overwhelmed by all this crap. Rosie's clever, and there was a camaraderie built between them during the whale rescue. I understand why she needed time before trusting me again. Ironically, I was just beginning to feel that I could totally trust her."

"Trust is important. Unfortunately, the rumors about you are downright vicious."

"I know! But how do you fight a whisper war? I've been reluctant to admit this because it's so embarrassing, but one of the rumors about me was pure projection. *Rosie* was the one that physically abused *me* during our last months together." Sky turned away from Dawn and looked out past the harbor before continuing.

"It started with a couple of screaming outbursts. Then she started throwing things, and finally she tried pounding on me when I was caught off-guard. She even slashed a painting at my studio."

"Oh, Sky, I had no idea you went through all that."

"In hindsight, her abuse kind of snuck up on me. For a while, it was just short outbursts. It was always about her unfounded suspicions. No matter how I tried to reassure her, it was never enough. Later, she really became violent. I *never* did anything to warrant that hostility."

"You should have called me."

"It became a matter of pride. I thought I could help her and it would all work out."

"Physical abuse by either side is far more common than reported," stated Dawn. "I admire you for keeping this private, but it must have been tough. I think Karina would have understood."

"Damn! Who the *hell* would believe me?" he said, feeling exasperated. "Rosie's so small! Maybe Karina would have understood, but it's a difficult subject to talk about."

"You should know that she desperately wants to see you, and hopes that you feel the same way."

"It's funny, just today I decided to call her. My life has been empty without her, and I've noticed that even my latest paintings seem to lack something. I wanted her to know the truth about my past relationship with Rosie."

Dawn stepped over to the porthole and looked toward the mouth of the harbor. A yellow submarine, armed with tons of tourists standing on the topside deck, entered the small harbor. She smiled at the sight.

"Sky, you were always one of the best things to come along in my life; you and Karina mean a lot to me. Someday, I'll probably need *you* for a bit of counseling. But now, there's about to be one ecstatic woman, who is now waiting, quite nervously, right around the corner at the Pioneer Inn. Need I say more?"

"Oh my God! Thanks, sweetie, for being a good friend at a critical time. I'll walk you out, and then go right over there. I've hoped for this moment, but now I'll have to clear my throat and... steady myself. I'm a little shaky."

"I'll let myself out. Good luck, you deserve it and you also deserve being with that sweet woman."

"Thanks again. I know that falling in love means taking risks. Just maybe — we're both ready."

Karina was sitting at a small table in the lounge of the 100 year-old Pioneer Inn. Five whaling harpoons were mounted vertically on the wall behind her, offering a throne-like regality to her setting. A large mural of three voluptuous nudes, relaxing on a sandy beach, hung on the same wall.

"Hello, sailor. Buy a girl a drink?" asked Karina. Her eyes held a twinkle and her smile suggested mischievous intention. Any whaler of yesteryear, coming through the swinging oak doors of the funky harbor bar, would have immediately steered a course toward the bright beacon in the corner.

"You look beautiful, kitten, may I kiss you first?"

"As long as you want." As Karina rose, Sky grabbed her and kissed her over and over. Tears slid down their cheeks, adding to their wet embrace. Pent-up passion flooded the regal corner. A table of fishermen watched briefly, but turned back to each other, an array of emotions written across their weathered, whiskered faces.

"I love you," said Sky softly.

"I love you, too. I'm sorry. I was so scared."

"I know. It's all right. Would you mind if a lonely sailor sat down?"

"We'd better before my wobbly legs give out."

"I'll get us a couple of beers," he said, catching his breath.

The bartender saw him coming and quickly popped a couple of cold ones.

"No charge," he said, handing Sky the beers. "You just reminded me of what I wish I'd done a long time ago."

By the time Sky returned, Karina had dried her face.

"That wonderful sparkle in your eyes has kept me awake at night," he said tenderly. "I haven't slept because I'm thinking of you all the time. I missed you more than you can possibly imagine."

"I was so frightened," Karina trembled. "She was so convincing. I know you couldn't do those things, but I've heard so many stories about lovers leading two lives, and... oh God, I should have trusted you. Can you forgive me?"

"I understood your reaction, but believed our

love would bring us back together. Now we'll be that much stronger. I love you. It's time for us to move forward." Sky looked into her eyes and felt the welling up of another flow of tears. He cleared his throat and looked up at the wall mural.

"I rented a room upstairs for a getaway weekend, sailor. Any chance you want to keep a lonely girl company?"

The sight of her pretended innocence and girlish charm made Sky laugh. His laugh was infectious and soon they were both laughing. The fishermen sneaked a peek, and one of them ordered a round of beers to be sent to their table. When the beers arrived, the anglers held their bottles up high and toasted the two lovers. Sky and Karina were still laughing as they raised their bottles in return.

FOWL FRONTIER

It was almost noon and a gale-like wind was whipping the daylights out of the 10,000-foot summit of Haleakala. Karina and Sky stood tenuously at the Sliding Sands trailhead, hoping the blinding downpour would soon clear. The torrent of rain pouring from Sky's safari hat reminded him of his shower massage on maximum jet spray. A shrouded trail snaked toward the bottom of the chilly chasm — well into the abyss. Three days of food and bedding rested on their backs.

"So *this* is our reward for winning two cabins in the lottery," kidded Sky. "Lucky us! They're at the bottom of the crater – somewhere. It's the pits, but let's slide into it," he joked with exaggerated exuberance.

"OK. But why do they call it 'the house of the sun'?"

"You'll see."

"At least we're heading down, because there's not much air up here."

"Honey, I would kiss those wet lips, but I'm afraid you'd suffocate."

"Go ahead, but remember I'm low on oxygen so hold the tongue."

After a wet embrace, Sky said, "Today's the summer solstice. You'll feel the heat when that short ray of sunlight bursts through. I'm betting your poncho will be off in 30 minutes, and if I'm wrong I'll carry your pack. Ha, ha, just kidding."

The rain was swirling upwards from the crater, so it was difficult to shield their faces from the cold spray.

"Savor the moment!" yelled Sky through the howling wind. "There's nothing like hiking down a slippery cinder trail with a 35-pound pack and a gale in your face. Ha, ha, right into the bowels of an active volcano. What could be more invigorating? Don't answer. I'll lead, and you can watch where I plant my feet."

"Sure. But I can't get too close, or that waterfall coming off your hat will sweep me away." She watched him begin the trudge toward the invisible floor of the energy-laden volcano. As he hiked down the slope, his limp was even more prominent. Karina made a mental note to get the full story of that limp; there would be plenty of time during the next three days.

Gratefully, they found a few isolated lava bombs alongside the path. The large boulders, polished and saddled by time, made convenient chairs and backrests for heavy packs. A long time ago, they were hurled into space from the depth of the eruption. The tephra chunks hardened during their lofty flight. The unique sculptures, spewed across the carpet of alpine shrubs, were reminders of Madame Pele's artwork.

A short time later the trail skirted a few silversword plants, and the sun broke through the storm. Large globules of water clung both to the silver stalks, and to the roseate petals showcased on the handsome silversword; the endangered species glistened in the splendor of isolated serenity.

"Oh, my goodness!" squealed Karina. "Look at this one! It's taller than you!"

"Careful, they're fragile."

The silversword was thick with dark red flowers resembling tiny daisies. Normally, the yucca-like plant sends up a flowering phallic spike only once in its lifetime and this for its swan song. It can wait 20 years before the virtuoso performance, withering away after the final curtain comes down.

"These tough characters are doing a little better lately," said Sky. "The goats and tourists were annihilating them. A fence was installed a few years ago for the goats. After that, they started trapping the tourists." He smiled mischievously, clearly gathering steam from the warm drying sun.

"With over a million visitors every year, no one missed a few. The rangers tossed the tourists into the 'Bottomless Pit.' Seriously, you have to admire the perseverance of the silversword, living up here in this barren wind-swept environment."

Some of the plants were clinging to the lava scree without any hint of real soil. Their roots were spread out just under the cinder floor to collect maximum moisture; their taproot kept them grounded.

"Well they must be lapping it up today after that monsoon. They're so precious, but I'm surprised even a goat would munch on those spiky stalks."

"Yeah, they're not exactly a tender-looking salad, but recently the combination of goats, pigs and mongoose came close to annihilating not only the silversword, but also the nene goose.

"Check out 'Pele's paint pot.' You can practically smell the cinders smoldering."

The small pit had a perfect circle of gray cinders wrapped over a cone of yellow sulfur and rust-iron. Waves of shadows washed across the painted pit, creating ominous patterns and darkening the mysteries below.

The harsh Aeolian environment softened. The clouds started to whiten and the air turned fresh and warm.

"It looks like the trail is about to level off," she said, grateful for the opportunity to revitalize her leg muscles and find a patch of moleskin for her big toe.

"Look," whispered Sky. "Near the bush. A nene. I heard the 'nay-nay' sound earlier. She's got a nest."

"Oh, poor baby, she looks nervous and drenched. Her babies are sure cute. Bless their hearts. Let's tiptoe past and wish them long life."

The nene family remained silent and the small goslings shivered from the recent downpour. Even without predators, this endangered goose was no happy camper, for this foul frontier was far from being fowl friendly.

They found Kapalaoa cabin deserted, except for the caretaker, a colorful gurgling goose. The male nene, looking for a handout, welcomed the hikers with his redundant and negative "nay-nay" cry. After hasty introductions with the caretaker, Sky and Karina collapsed on the cabin steps.

"I guess we have our watch-goose tonight," said Karina. "He seems to know his way around this charming lodge. Black neckband, black head, he looks like a bandit. Check out his black leggings." She looked up and surveyed the alien terrain. The cabin was nestled against the bottom of a 1000-foot craggy wall, and from the refuge she could see most of the crater floor, featuring a variety of giant, conical mounds.

"My gosh! This setting is extraordinary," she sighed. "We have a full panorama of those cinder cones. It's a perfect place to watch the fireworks — just kidding. They're not going to release any pent-up energy tonight, are they?"

"I think the odds are low," he replied as he unlocked the cabin door. "Shall I stick a fake log in the stove?"

"Sure. How do they bring up the supplies?"

"Helicopter and pack horse. We have to conserve our fuel and water. After we break the chill in here, let's sit outside and watch the full-moon show."

The cabin had a stark, utilitarian ambience. The floor was worn smooth from thousands of tired feet. The metal bunk beds were military and cold, but a couple of warm logs transformed the primitive cabin into a cozy home.

"Let me grab my parka," said Karina.

"Yeah, then let's wander around our homestead. Speaking of wandering about, we only have bunks for ten 'night marchers,' if they insist on stopping over."

"OK, OK! No snipe and no night marcher stories tonight. I really need to relax my aching muscles. The merlot should help. Where's the corkscrew, Ranger Sky?"

"Coming."

"I can't wait to sit outside and talk story with Gabby Goose. It sure gets dark early in this hole. Not that I'm complaining. The sky is clear and the guide is quite handsome."

"Handsome, huh. Allow me to prepare the entrée for this evening. Tonight we will savor the cuisine of the northern Italian Riviera. I will prepare from scratch, a can of the finest spaghetti to ever reach the innards of this volcanic pit."

"Oh angel, you are sooo romantic. Slaving over a hot can of spaghetti confirms your gallant culinary talent. Allow me to give the chef a big kiss. Cheers! Let's hope the moon shows up for our solstice party."

Later, the parkas and the merlot warmed the evening chill that surrounded the steps. Behind the cabin, a high ridge blocked part of the night sky, delaying the grand entrance of the full moon.

Finally, the fat silver orb emerged and immediately put on a performance worthy of this moon-like terrain. Like lasers, silver streaks splayed across the fire-fed floor, and playful white lights danced behind swirling black clouds. The moon seemed to be sucked into a series of fast moving clouds, like a genie sucked back into his bottle.

"There aren't many stars yet," Karina observed, "but it seems fitting that we have my young vivacious Venus and your old manly Mars watching over us. Two polarized planets sharing the sky. It's magical here. I love you, angel. I'm so sorry I ever doubted you. What was I thinking?"

"I can't imagine a more powerful place on earth to reunite," replied Sky, "assuming this is actually earth. I love you, too. Maybe it's time to go in and warm up. Top or bottom?"

"Bottom bunk. Hopefully that's what you meant, right next to your warm furry body."

They carefully climbed into one of the lower bunks. Sky snuggled up to Karina to form the spooning position. Naked, they cuddled in a fetal embrace, pressing every reachable pore together. The double sleeping bag provided warmth and security.

The rhythm of their breathing harmonized and

after a time, quieted. They became one. They returned to the womb, returned to mother earth. Exhausted, they slept in the quiet crater capsule, secure in their cabin, snug in their bag.

In the middle of the night, nature called; Sky bundled up and walked across the squeaky wood floor. Outside, the sights and sounds were surreal. He quickly forgot the purpose of his nocturnal mission and hurried back.

"Wake up. You won't believe what's happening outside," he whispered into Karina's ear and then gently kissed her warm forehead. After she bundled up, he carefully led her into the chill of the night.

"Oh, my gosh! What's all the ruckus?"

"Birds," Sky replied with a short laugh. "Mostly petrels partying on the mountainside. They fly up here from the beach and nest at night. It sounds like they're fighting, but they're just celebrating the summer solstice. Can you believe a few crater cavorters can make that racket?"

"No. The noise sounds eerie in this desolate place, and yet it was so quiet earlier. Don't you think it's spooky, all those yips and groans?"

"It shows we're not alone in this giant pit," said Sky pensively.

"Let's not be forgetting Gabby Goose."

"Of course. Let's get back before we freeze to death. Oh, and give me an extra minute. I just remembered why I came out here in the first place."

They could still hear the dark-rumped songsters wailing through the cabin walls. The hard-rock band partied until dawn.

CATCHING A RAINBOW

"Time to greet the day," announced Sky. "I've got these pressed logs heating up the Swedish pancakes. They should warm you up on this foggy morning."

"If you were my true hero, you'd go outside and pee for me." Half-asleep, she staggered outside; the open sleeping bag bunched up over her head.

"I'm glad you didn't come through the door in the middle of the night, looking like the mummy from the bottomless pit," said Sky, flipping the first miniature pancake.

She returned with the bag draped over her shoulder. "What's that? They're out of Norwegian pancakes at Safeway? You know our clan prefers the hearty Viking pancakes over those little Swedish things. Hey, they're just the size for Gabby. Ha-ha, just teasing.

"Actually, I really appreciate waking up to the smell of coffee. And watching you slave over a hot stove in those sexy shorts is kind of stimulating too. After coffee, I want you to tell me the story of your limp. I know you said it was a long time ago."

"Yeah, the worst time of my life. So far, only Buddy knows the true story of what happened, but I guess it's time you knew too.

"One night I witnessed this guy beating up a woman. Nobody else was around. She was screaming like crazy, and naturally I ran over. When I got there I could see she was bleeding bad and trying to defend herself. The next thing I knew the guy turned on me, and I was fighting for my life.

"I don't remember much. Even the woman was hitting me. The guy was throwing me against this wall. Finally, rage took over and I literally threw him through the air. His head hit the pole of a streetlight and he died on the spot. That crazy woman kept screaming at me until the police arrived. Later, she testified against me." Sky narrowed his eyes. Hard furrows terraced down his forehead.

"I ended up serving three years in jail. My leg was shattered from the fight, and it was never set properly. I have this limp as a memory."

Karina stared at him in shock. Then her face softened and she started crying. He held her tightly while she sobbed on his chest. It took awhile before she could talk. She was thinking about the impact on him, along with the memory of her own disillusive youth.

"Oh, Sky! You of all people. You're so gentle."

"It was a long time ago, kitten. Twenty years. I try not to pay attention to stuff happening on the street anymore. It was a lesson in life, a lose-lose lesson."

"You've obviously handled it well. I would never have guessed."

"Yeah, thanks. I hope you're right."

Sky knew that Buddy and Karina would never reveal his secret, but he worried that Rosie would discover it. He was glad he had given his revengeful ex-girlfriend, along with everyone else, the African lion version for his limp.

Switching moods, he joked, "Are you ready for face to face combat with the fog outside?"

"Soon as I pack the maple syrup."

A thick cool mist accompanied their dawn march to Paliku cabin. Reaching a small hill on the trail, they looked over the standing fog and marveled at a glowing surface of fresh snow on the Big Island's distant peaks, Mauna Loa and Mauna Kea. The peaks seemed to float atop the cloudbank.

The eastern side of the crater floor turned lush. Two-hundred inches of rain a year kept the trees and greenery thriving.

Twenty minutes later it poured. Visibility reached zero. There was no refuge and the trail quickly became a stream. Karina slipped and fell and then Sky went down.

They stood again, clinging to each other and shouted encouragement back and forth through the wet hell. The wind increased and they both fell into the sodden, slippery muck. There was concern that the flood might wash them toward Kaupo Gap.

"I know it's not a 'moleskin moment,' but I think my leg's bleeding," yelled Sky above the howling gale. "Don't worry, we'll be fine."

"I know, but my ankle hurts and I feel like a drenched rat. How can a tropical island be so damn cold?"

The heavy rain stopped just as quickly as it had started. Feeling blessed, they trudged on toward the shelter.

"It's a wild place — one minute vibrant, another violent," said Sky. "How ironic if we were washed away by a flood in a dormant volcano."

"And as if I needed more respect for the energy of this beautiful mountain," said Karina.

Paliku cabin rose from the bog like a welcome mirage. They were soon warm from the fire in the stove; dry clothes from their waterproof packs added more warmth to their spirits. Their minor injuries were taped and forgotten for the moment.

Later in the evening, they ventured outside. As they strolled across the wet meadow, the cabin appeared cozy and safe. The fast-flying clouds had thinned and the rain was in recess. Smoke from the chimney drifted across the peak of the roof.

"Look!" yelled Sky. "You can see Alpha Centauri. And the Southern Cross!"

"Beautiful," she gasped, admiring the view from inside the eye of the storm. "It's worth the price of admission even though the Southern Cross is slightly askew. It feels like we're hanging on the edge of the moon, literally, and watching the world go by."

Silently a star slipped from the sky. More likely, a meteor fragment burned through the atmosphere. Willowy waterfalls tumbled over the top of the ridge behind the cabin and down the creviced crater wall. A magical interlude prevailed in the belly of the mythical mountain, and they returned to the cabin in awe.

Then, once again, the rain pelted the plateau and peppered their tin roof. The rhythmic heavy metal drumming discouraged quiet cabin conversation; they turned to their paperbacks.

"Tomorrow will be one long slog through the bog," said Sky. He sensed nature's poetry on a long summer's night inside the volcanic house of Pele.

In the morning, sun filtered through the cabin windows,

giving incentive for an early start.

Akala, the giant native raspberry, thrived in the soggy soil directly behind the cabin. Gigantic woodferns, like huge green shuttlecocks, flourished in the nurturing crotch of trees in the direction of Kaupo Gap, and the purple-berried Hawaiian Hawthorne prospered in lush lifestyle.

Native red lehua flowers glorified the cabin surroundings, along with meadows of tall grass, shrubs, and varietal ferns.

"These sweet raspberries will be perfect for our morning brunch," said Karina. "I can't believe this soggy soil. What happened to 'Madame Cinder Land?' My boot tops are barely over this muck."

"Well den, let's jus' get da muck atta here," said Sky, feeling vigor from the sunny morning that belied his jesting. "We'll be back to the barren zone in a couple of hours, so enjoy the greenery. What shall we talk about during our ten-mile uphill trek?"

"Tell me some more secrets about yourself and your friends."

"You sure you want to know?" asked Sky reluctantly. "All right, maybe a mythical mountain is the place to share a few things. Of course, the whole island is threaded with secrets, probably the binding that keeps this island afloat."

"Remember the food-bank booth at the taro festival?" she asked. "Tell me why you didn't talk about your involvement."

"I'm part of the financial wing of the food bank, although it's the dedicated volunteers who deserve the credit. Last year, we came up with the idea of getting all the condos to collect leftover food from departing tourists. It's added 500 cans to our monthly program.

"My finance method is somewhat of a secret, but it's really a win-win deal. I have a few dozen wealthy patrons that I contact by email and announce a charity auction for one of my paintings. The highest bidder writes a check to the organization, and I have a contract for one dollar with the patron. They get the tax write-off and we all win, perfectly legal. One of four paintings has this special purpose.

"I'm impressed."

"The best part is that I enjoy painting. Only two officers know my involvement. As you know, I'm more comfortable with a low profile, although a few times a year I help out at the distribution center when they get overwhelmed."

"I'm blown away, but since you love your art, it seems like the perfect contribution. I'd like to help out at the food bank."

"We can always use the help."

Dark clouds gathered before them as they hobbled uphill. A magnificent rainbow appeared within the crater confines, framing the mineral-rich pastel hills. There were tints of gold, charcoal, sandy-gray, silver and mossy-green to admire. For an instant the crater held more vibrant colors than one of Sky's canvases.

"Wow, it's a double-bow!" exclaimed Karina. "There's two complete circles of color touching the ground!"

"Yeah, and it's coming closer! *It's incredible!* Let's see if we can reach the end."

"I can't believe we have our boots inside the colors," said Karina. "That's a first for me."

"Me too. Not often do you chase a rainbow and actually catch it. Must be a sign of good luck." Before disappearing, the colorful concentric arches fused and slowly faded away, like the memory of a distant relationship.

"Tell me more secrets. It'll take my mind off my aching ankle and sore shoulder."

"You want more secrets, huh? OK, but only for medicinal purposes. Let's see. You know Gecko, the little Japanese lady who gave you a massage in Hana? Well, she had an affair with a 15-year-old surfer. She looks about 15, so I guess no one noticed.

"And Liz, our Wailea socialite, inherited a lot of her money from hotdogs. Her extended family is Oscar Mayer. She used some of the money to set up a highly profitable celebrity escort service in Washington, D.C. The city gave her a choice of jail or leave town. She chose exile in an outpost called Maui, and now spends most of her time lying around the Grand Wailea Spa and playing monopoly with her real estate." Karina slowed her pace.

"Then, there's our overgrown and crusty Buddy. He always ends up with the sexiest woman on the dance floor, and is one of the smoothest tango dancers on the island. He keeps his twinkle toes a secret.

"Gabe, my other good pal, who you'll get to meet at the luau, has lived with an alcoholic wife for years. She rarely ventures out, so not many people know about her condition."

He ended his diatribe by saying, "Rosie, our good Samaritan, was a teen prostitute. How's that?" He looked away. He was drained and suddenly very uncomfortable.

Karina stared at him wondering what to say. Her own life had certainly not been sheltered, and there was little that ever shocked her. But hearing all of this in the same breath stunned her. She realized that Sky had made his comments without judgment, but now he seemed to regret his outburst.

"Is it all true?" she asked.

"As far as I know. I know you won't tell anyone about this stuff, and it gives you a little more insight into these characters. Man, I feel awkward now. You know my feelings about rumors."

"Then tell me about Rosie," she said tenderly.

"Rosie had a tough childhood. Her father abandoned her when she was 12. Her mother walked out on her when she was 16, and she had to completely fend for herself. One particular girlfriend had a strong influence, and with her friend's prodding, Rosie turned tricks to support herself for about a year. After that she took an interest in animals and resumed school classes. The rest is history."

"But those teen years probably explain why she has this weird revengeful side. She needs professional help."

Karina smiled, "You've definitely taken my mind off the pain in my ankle with your tidbits. Shall we continue the journey? I have lots to mull over."

"What's your big secret?" asked Sky, hopeful his maligning revelations would not require further detail during rest of the hike.

"As far as my big secret... it's that I'm in love with you angel, but maybe it's not much of a secret." It didn't seem like a good time for her to mention the small technicality of being secretly married.

"I think it's far easier to start a rumor," continued Karina, "than to keep a secret on this island. Don't worry. Your comments will always be safe with me."

"I suppose we all have our secrets," he said soberly. "Now all that's left is climbing the 1000-foot switchback trail."

"Ugh!"

"Those dark clouds should hold, and for incentive there's a liquid surprise in the trunk of the car. But, you'll need to get a good grip on your vertigo along the way. Shall we have a race?"

"Yeah," she replied. "We'll call it the 'Gimpy vs. Limpy Run to the Sun.' How about a sendoff kiss before the great race?"

"Absolutely. On your mark...."

SILENT SPEAR

The world-class freediver glided at a depth of ten feet below the ocean surface. It was easy for Buddy and Joni to track their friend, Gabe Cabalo, with the overhead sun blazing through the sparkling blue water. Gabe was "shopping" for Buddy's upcoming lu'au in the world's biggest and freshest fish market.

In spear fishing, there are no bubbles to alarm fish. It's stealth hunting — underwater.

"Do you think we have enough?" asked Joni. "The big cooler is almost full."

"We get plenty ono fish fo' da party," said Buddy, "an' plenty pig from da hunt last month. Now dat Sky an' his sweetie back again, hope everyone can chill wit' dea mates fo' one mo' week."

"I'm not going anywhere," said Joni, "especially when you keep inviting me out on the Lucky Strike. I like being chief cook and bottle washer for your boat trips. Cleaning fish makes me puke, but you've already discovered my *special* talent."

"Yeah baby, dat's why dis lu'au goin' be jus' special fo' you," he said as Gabe surfaced again.

"You look all pau," Buddy yelled down to Gabe. "I t'ink we plenty fish fo' da party already."

Gabe slid his mouthpiece to the side. The sun

reflected off his shiny, bald head. "There's some kids in Waikapu that always see me comin'," he panted. "They like wait fo' me when I comin' wit' the fish. I goin' try get couple mo' fo' them. You guys gettin' too hot?"

"No worry 'bout us," said Buddy. "You spear em, we chill em. Dat last mahimahi was one big beaut."

"Yeah, thanks for your boat today. Makes way mo' easy da spear fishin'. It's too deep here for anchor, and my Zodiac always drift away. Spend plenty time chasin' after her in dis rough channel."

Gabe was also grateful that Buddy was there to pull off the fish from his spear gun. Normally, he had to string his catch and they would dangle from a flag-mounted orange buoy; a long line connected it to the end of his gun. Sometimes he lost part of his catch to predators, and twice he lost his entire catch to freeloading sharks. During those two events the line seemed far too short.

Today he was testing a brand new spear gun. It had a beautifully carved teak barrel, twin black cocking rubbers, and a bayonet front mount. Powerful, maneuverable, and stealth silent, it featured the latest in high technology. Hardened stainless steel shafts and spearpoints controlled the accuracy of flight.

"Go for it, Gabe, you seem to have a lucky spot here," said Joni. "We'll do a quality test on a couple Buds while we're waiting, just to make sure they stay cold enough."

"I show her how I open em wit' two teeth," said Buddy, playfully. A surprised look came over Joni and Gabe laughed.

"You children can figure sometin' fo' keep busy," Gabe teased. He replaced his mouthpiece. Most of the next dives would be successful, and the stocky diver would average nearly three minutes of downtime.

"Besides Sky and Karina, who's coming to the party?" asked Joni.

"Course Gabe comin'. He good pal. I already told you dat he paddles on da Makena Masters team wit' me and Sky, but he also help build da Moloka'i fishpond wit' Sky each month. Maybe he bring his wife Angelina, if she sober enough for come. Poor guy — plenty years gotta live wit' alcoholic wife. If she come, you fo' sure goin' find her at da bar."

"That's a shame. He's such a great guy. I knew he had three teenage girls, but I had no idea about his wife. They must keep it secret."

"Dey try. She no go out too much. She was in AA and he go Al-Anon. Dey like try rehab couple times, but nothin' work. But she good woman wit' da kids. He jus' no let her go out at night. He love her, but I know he like plenty deprived in mo' ways den one."

Gabe surfaced and lifted his mask up, the mouthpiece of his snorkel dangling over his ear. He was breathing hard.

"Ten minutes mo' and I'm pau," he gasped between breaths.

"No need worry, we no go nowhere," joked Buddy.

"Thanks. In case sun fry you' brain and you no can remember me, I maybe make swim fo' Lana'i in 'bout ten hours. Betta we no find out. Next time come up be plenty ready fo' one cold one. Need it after pullin' this tough 'rubber' back, and gettin' my shoulder whacked wit' all the kicks." He took in a huge breath, blew most of it out and with one powerful kick dove straight down.

"Dawn Paris comin,'" continued Buddy. "Some of da paddlers on our team, a few neighbors, and some tango classmates say dey goin' be dea. It's gonna be real sweet showin' you off to da gang. You goin' like everyone. Jus' no tell da fishermen dat you lua'i when clean da fish."

"Ah, but I have other skills. Maybe they don't know how to 'jerk' a wild boar or prepare an orgasmic lavender drink," Joni giggled, "or guarantee that the captain of the Lucky Strike gets *real* lucky when I'm aboard. Unless of course, there's company. Anyway, I can't wait to meet your friends."

They watched as Gabe came up and reloaded a spear after missing a 60-pound ulua.

"Maybe still down there," he gasped with a determined look. He dove quickly and followed in the direction of the prized Hawaiian fish.

"Look!" yelled Joni, as she recognized the unmistakable dorsal fin slice through the surface. With its indomitable oscillating motion, the powerful body charged directly at Gabe.

"Oh shit, it's a *shark*!" yelled Buddy.

"Gabe! Gabe! Gabe!" yelled Joni.

"He no can hear! I'll bang da side of da boat. Oh no, it's almost on him! Shit, it's a tiger!"

They watched as the tail fin powered the predator toward Gabe, who was nearly motionless in ten feet of water. The blunt head and blurred gray tiger-like markings across the top of the thick skin made it easy to identify. The attacking tiger shark was twice the size of Gabe's six-foot spear gun.

Gabe had followed the ulua, but his slippery target had vanished. He had allowed his body to drift back into an upright position and now he waited. His gun was cocked and pointed toward the empty sea. He felt something funny on the back of his neck and turned around. The tiger shark came straight at his face — jaws wide open. The teeth were curved and serrated — and terrifying. The sight of the lower cutting choppers was enough to paralyze most prey with fright. Gabe never moved, not even an inch.

"He sees him!" shouted Joni. Her jaw dropped and her mouth opened wide. Her face showed shock and fear, unlike the raw menacing look of the shark. "Shoot him, do something. Oh my God!"

Gabe had only one thing to do; his spear gun was already "shoulder-ready" in anticipation of shooting the ulua. When he turned, he could see the giant jaws coming straight at him. There was no need to aim. He pulled the trigger, and the gun kicked back hard into his shoulder. The four-foot steel-tipped spear traveled only twelve inches from the end of his gun; *twelve inches* that would be remembered by both diver and witnesses for the rest of their lives.

The entire metal shaft went down the tiger's throat; the force stopped the charge of the predator dead in his wake. The tiger sank immediately, and Gabe quickly cut his spear line. He wanted no further part of this lethal fish, which was both revered and feared in the community.

When Gabe surfaced, he was as calm as ever. He looked more concerned about the loss of his ulua than nearly becoming the shark's lunch.

"Jesus, Gabe, look like you a goner! Musta had less than a second, you!"

"Gabe, you all right?" cried Joni.

Gabe removed his mask and moved over to the diver's platform.

"I'm fine. I need let 'em go. Must think plenty long before bring shark aboard. Right now, one cold beer sounds ono."

Gabe drank his beer in silence. Buddy also kept quiet, while Joni talked non-stop. She described the danger over and over. Finally, with the salt washed from his throat and his thoughts sorted, Gabe spoke.

"I've seen plenty sharks, and they all take good look at me. I t'ink we both get plenty respect. Tiger only one 'round here that attacks people. I understand how the Hawaiian people honor sharks 'cause many ways they beautiful.

"But locals talk 'bout renegades in all the species, includin' sharks. We know it from our own — the one black sheep. Even reincarnation has chance that evil spirit lurkin' in the species." Gabe swallowed the rest of his beer.

"I believe that shark was chasing the same ulua, and when look at me t'ink I jus' one mo' fish. It's nature and it's pau. I feel bad, but I have...." He choked as he continued, "but I have a family at home." He looked out to sea. "We got mo' beer?"

"Hell yes!" said Buddy, "I get one ice cold. We need plenty big toast here."

Joni leaped over to Gabe and hugged him. She was soon sobbing on his shoulder.

"When Joni's pau, I like give you hug," said Buddy, trying to check his emotions.

"Dey eat everythin' you know," reflected Gabe. "They're the garbage shark of the ocean and eat everythin', includin' the kitchen sink, if they find one. True. In those stomachs already find seabirds, cows, goats, dogs and human parts. Also find small anchors, bolts, and nails in dem iron bellies. You like can start hardware store wit' jus' one tiger."

"No wonder he sank so fast," kidded Joni, "with *that* heavy diet. Oh, Gabe, I'm so glad you're OK. I still have the shakes."

Gabe laughed. "I gonna get plenty shakes comin' before we get back. Cheers, mates!"

"Cheers!" Buddy and Joni yelled simultaneously.

BUDDY'S BASH

"It happened to our team during a crew change," said Karina. "It was so rough that most of the time we couldn't see their canoe; even the escort boat kept disappearing behind those huge white waves. Then the canoe *and* the escort boat got swamped and sank! They both sank! Just like that! We were on Lookout Point with binoculars and all of a sudden all the guys were swimming in the ocean trying to survive monster waves."

Karina and Joni had the rapt attention of all the women who were sitting in the carport at Buddy's annual luau. They were telling the story of last week's Great Kahakuloa Canoe Race from Kahului to Lahaina.

Karina and Joni had shadowed the 16-team canoe race in Joni's Ford Ranger around the north end of the island; their attention focused on Sky, Buddy, and Gabe in the Makena outrigger canoe. They had to drive quickly along the curvy coastal road in order to catch the canoes passing below the cliffs.

Canoe groupies gathered at every major lookout point along the course, and the remote cliffs became cheering bleachers for boisterous fans. Roars of encouragement would echo down the craggy cliffs and out to sea as a pair of binoculars picked out their team's canoe. A few of the groupies grabbed their cell phones and tried to make contact, but most of them were content to munch on goodies from the ABC Store.

The cliff parties lasted only a few brief minutes before the canoes raced past, and all the groupies once again jumped into their pickups. Then the scenic vistas returned to their serenity, except for the whistling sound of wind.

"My God, they sank?" burst out Dawn.

"Everyone on the point was screaming," said Joni. "A few of the kids were crying. Karina and I were shattered. Those guys looked like tiny corks getting tossed around. We felt helpless."

"To make matters worse, our team was so far ahead of the second place Kihei crew that the ocean looked empty through our binoculars," said Karina. "Just knowing there were all those paddlers trying to tread water in giant waves with no boat around ...."

"Luckily, someone on the Kihei escort boat saw what happened and they raced to the rescue," said Joni. "In ten minutes they were picking up our team."

"Sky, Buddy, and Gabe had been getting ready to jump out for the crew change when a wave buried them and their outrigger," said Karina. "The relief crew was already in the water waiting to climb aboard, when another huge wave crashed over the escort boat, and *it* flipped over and sank."

Joni said, "Buddy hasn't talked about it much. It would have been their first masters' division win in the Kahakuloa."

"The captain is a good friend of his," Karina added. "Right now the captains of both of those escorts are aboard Buddy's boat in the backyard, getting wined and dined by our intrepid paddlers."

Dawn looked incredulous. The story played into her worse nightmare. She expressed the same thought of many women in the carport when she said, "Lucky they weren't in last place."

The carports of North Kihei served their residents in many ways, but sheltering a car was as unlikely as spotting a snake. Sometimes, the simple framed structures were filled to the roof with storage. More likely, the residents kept some of the carport cleared for a few chairs or a picnic table. Shade, fresh air, and cold beer softened the sight of weed-whackers and gasoline cans. Carport and party place meant the same in this community.

The informality made it easy to talk story, pick at pupu, and swat bloody mosquitoes. Attention sometimes diverted to a streaking cockroach, the sharp clacking call of a gabby gecko, or the ear-splitting sound of a roving family of francolins. The francolin family's call was the most difficult to ignore; one bird alone had the same chilling pitch as the war cry of a band of Indians, charging around the circled wagon trains of yesteryear.

Buddy had spent part of the morning hosing off the thick agricultural dust and black "Maui snow" (cane-burn ash) from his carport. After which, he powdered the oil spots in preparation for his annual summer luau, known to his friends as "Buddy's Bash." The old corroded refrigerator was crammed with drinks.

The overall appearance of North Kihei was a tropical hodgepodge, and Buddy Kanoa's backyard blended nicely into this jumble of beach shacks and low-cost housing developments. The rear of the large lot served as the final resting home for his former trucks; prolific weeds kept them surrounded in companionship. Odd bits of metal and wood occupied a good portion of the yard, although it was possible to carefully meander through the maze of junk.

A long concrete slab wandered off toward the rear of the yard. At the end, Buddy's beloved 30-foot adventure boat glistened in a backlight of afternoon sun and reigned supreme over the large junkyard. Majestically, it rose from the cluttered weed patch, like the sphinx rising above the barren desert.

On the other side of the carport, a kapu sign warned of the underground charcoal pit, which was cooking the pig ever so slowly. Some of Buddy's guests were gathered on the runway, but most of the women were in the carport sitting in plastic four-dollar Home Depot chairs and talking story. The guys were nautically high and dry, swapping tales in the cockpit of the Lucky Strike.

Aboard the boat, Buddy finished telling the story of the shark attack to the guys sitting on the aft cockpit.

"And dat's wat happen," said Buddy. "Eh, Gabe, like add mo?'"

"Dis all plenty heavy wit' local legend," Gabe said. "Betta show respect for the shark by no talk 'bout it. Give 'em peace." Gabe didn't mention that he would be in those same waters next weekend.

The guys weren't sharing his sentiment, and one paddler jokingly called him the "Portagee man-of-war." Gabe laughed louder than anyone at the ethnic reference. He offered to tell the story about his friend's ghost, hoping to change the subject.

Hawaiian ghost stories are legendary. Nearly every local person and a good deal of old-time kama'ainas on Maui knew of a personal story. Besides the usual batch of ghost stories, Hawai'i enchants with local Menehune stories, legends about former forest dwellers that were not much taller than four feet.

The muscular elves had a reputation for building major projects, such as fishponds, in one night without ever being seen. Unexplained events on Maui were often thought to be the work of the mischievous Menehune.

The uniquely Hawaiian stories of the Night Marchers are quite different and far more sobering. Ghostly Night Marchers haunt certain Maui areas at night and often have a set path. Their torches have been seen as they march at night in single file. Drumming is often heard before the line of ghostly torches comes into view.

Their purpose is to recreate marches to old battlegrounds and pay tribute to either the fallen warriors or the noble ali'i from long ago. They allow no disturbance from mortals along the path, and witnesses must quickly turn away and never look into a marcher's eye. Standing, even innocently, on their path risks death or forced entry into their ghostly warrior family.

Personal Night Marcher tales abound on Maui and many sightings and drumming sounds have been reported around the island, especially near the coast. The area from Waiehu to Lahaina is a favorite haunt, where many bloody battles took place.

"The ghost was sittin' top his chest wen he was sleepin'. Really, it's the truth," said Gabe. Not one of the guys doubted his story for a minute.

"I saw what happened!" Gabe's eyes grew large as he continued. "We were campin' in Iao Valley. Small group. My friend, he sleepin' under the stars longside my tent. In the middle of the night, I hear screamin', 'get off me, get off me!' I grab one flashlight and jump outside. Wit' nothin' over him, he jus' lyin' there. His body pushed down, like way into his sleeping pad, but his chest — *oh my God* — it was scary. His chest all sunk in, like one big boulder sittin' on it! What to do? Could only watch.

"Finally, he sucked one loud breath and turned on his side. He neva sleep rest of night. I know cause he move in my tent and spend all night sittin' up and starin' at the tent zipper. Everyone say it was one of the Night Marchers, maybe one warrior killed from battle. Sky know 'bout these t'ings."

"You guys know I don't like talking about this stuff," said Sky. "Gabe is connected to the spiritual world and we should believe him. I'll say a couple of things, and then I think we should change topics, especially as it's getting dark.

"There was plenty of brutal slaughter at the battles of Iao Valley, and I know that valley has always been regarded as spiritual and ghostly ground. I've hiked there many times, but never overnight. The energy there is as strong as that of Haleakala." Sky paused and studied his beer bottle for a while. When he finally spoke, his voice was softer and his words were slower.

"Night Marchers get upset if someone blocks their path, and I think Gabe's friend was fortunate. Most believers would say that another marcher from the guy's former family came to his rescue just in time."

He continued, returning to his normal tone and rhythm. "The other thing is that I've been living with a ghost for the past few months. It's just your garden variety friendly spirit announcing a presence.

At least once a month, while I'm taking a leak in the bathroom, a loud tap hits the shower curtain next to me. *Right* next to me! I can see a large bulge in one part of the curtain about the size of a human head, and believe me, it's not the wind or anything else. There's actually a thud. By the time I look behind the curtain there's nothing but an empty shower. Truthfully, I've grown fond of the company, but wish I knew its identity or its purpose."

"Eh, Sky, you said it!" said Buddy hurriedly. Time we talk story wit' sometin' else." Everyone quickly agreed and someone asked Sky to tell the lion story.

"Half you guys already heard it. Oh, all right." He feigned a look of frustration.

"I had been at a safari camp for five days, and every day my newfound buddy, who was a former guide in Zimbabwe, insisted on taking me out to find a lion. Well, we had to get up long before sunrise to reach the lake by dawn. This guy was totally frustrated at not finding a lion, but on the fifth morning he spotted a male strolling by the lake. It was so dark you could barely see him from the jeep window.

"The next thing I knew, he yelled for me to get out and run. Suddenly I was chasing a huge male lion! We actually chased him for some distance along the side of the lake before he bounded away, but I went flying over a branch and broke a bone in my lower leg. The local clinic tried to set it, but it never healed properly. That's how I got the limp."

"I see," said one of the paddlers. "You attacked a lion! Did you have a mental lapse, or are you really nuts?"

"Caught up in the moment, I'm afraid. My crazy

friend had been guiding for 20 years. Later, he told me the lion *might* have already eaten."

Buddy shook his head and laughed. "Haole boy chase lion, catch broken leg." He knew the story was true, except the part about the broken leg. It was a good cover story for his pal.

One of the boys asked Buddy about his girlfriend Joni, posing the question in a lecherous and conspiratorial manner. Soon there was a chorus of beer drinkers demanding the scoop on Buddy's girl.

"You guys goin' meet her, but you betta watch yo' freakin' manners," growled Buddy. Sky volunteered to get more beer for the group.

At the carport, Sky decided to grab the entire cooler. He waved to the women and winked at Karina. Karina smiled back and blew him a kiss. Someone kidded him about paddling in a race without a canoe, drawing laughter from the others. Most of the women continued to stare at him as he picked up the heavy cooler and strode off.

As soon as Sky left, the women flattered him and congratulated Karina. Unfortunately, one of the women asked Karina if she'd heard the rumors about Sky, unaware that Karina was all too familiar with them. Karina acknowledged hearing them and suggested she consider the source. Quickly, someone changed the subject. Karina looked unconcerned, but below the surface she felt the stinging pain of public humiliation.

Meanwhile, Sky handed up the cooler to the "backyard salts." From dry-dock they were regaling their stories of the high seas.

"Sky, can you give hand wit' da pig?" asked Buddy. "I see Joni gettin' da BBQ ready fo' da fish. Rest you guys can climb down in 'bout 20 minutes.

Mr. Shafer's porker should be pau and ready for da gran' unveilin'."

On the way over to the pit, Buddy put his arm around Sky. He knew there was never a good time to talk about stuff like the caustic "dirt" he heard in his last tango class. He figured that he could spit it out, keep it short, and maybe quit thinking about the contemptible thing.

"Listen, ole pal, you no get crazy now, but one of da gals in my dance class say when you wit' Rosie, you wen' abuse her. That's one bad rap. But, betta you know wat I hear."

Sky did not answer immediately. Then he exploded. "Buddy, you should know better! For some perverted reason, that woman is out to ruin my life, and she's turned the facts completely around."

"OK, settle down. I believe you, but dis kinda crap no go too well in dis town. You need muzzle her, maybe get one attorney. Your buds may believe you, but all dis talk can get to some of dem."

"Yeah, yeah, I may just do that," said Sky trying to hold back his outrage. "Goddamn it, you *know* I'm not confrontational! And of all people, you know damn why. I keep thinking this bullshit will blow over, or maybe she will blow herself up."

"Sorry 'bout all dis shit; maybe betta I saved it fo' odda time," said Buddy. "I jus' neva like see you catch off guard. Now we go forget dis freakin' gossip and try diggin' up your beast. I got good mitts here fo' peelin' off da wrap, but tradition say we need burn our hands."

"All right," agreed Sky. Although he was seething, he was determined to fake it through the rest of the party. He believed he was being torn apart, limb by limb, in a war of attrition. But how could he fight whispers? One thing was clear. Whispers on Maui could shatter the lives of islanders. It was time to plan a counterattack.

The boisterous boat brigade came over, and then the rest of the party gathered around the pit. Gabe was asked to give a ceremonial blessing before the pig was unwrapped. Then Buddy and Sky donned the heavy mitts and peeled away the ti leaves and burlap. It didn't take long before a squeal of pain rang out. Sky jerked his exposed wrist away from the wrap as Karina raced to get cold water. Jokes flooded across the pit area as rapidly as the quick chop of a breezy sea.

"Tusker's last stand," kidded one of the guys.

"Your wrist looks done to perfection," teased one of the women.

"Sure your house ghost ain't no ugly old pig?" suggested someone from the boat party. Sky was soon laughing with all the others. The scrumptious smell of steamy kalua pork spread throughout the crowd. Joni returned to the BBQ area just in time to chase off a couple of neighbor cats creeping up on the fish. Dawn decided it was time to unwrap the bowls of food on the picnic table, and everyone hurried over to help themselves.

MANGO MEDICINE

Despite her advanced age of twelve, Mango prided herself on the fact that she wasn't just another beautiful orange tabby with a long, silky coat. Under her soft fluff, sinewy muscles waited for the opportunity to demonstrate her lightening speed.

Ever the hunter, she loved to leap onto the drapes and chase lame-headed lizards up and down the delicate cloth. Startled flies were plucked from midair. Her favorite sport, though, was felling sparrows. A camouflage of potted flowers on the fifth-story lanai provided a sparrow-blind to launch her attacks.

She didn't consider her long drawn-out "release and catch" game one of torment; she thought of it as one of fair play with plenty of opportunities for her dazed opponent. Piling feathers on top of a bird's bloody head, and leaving the flighty leftovers on the off-white Berber carpet, gave testament to her youthful agility, as did the trophy tail of a lizard.

In terms of human longevity and despite her prowess, she was Rosie's elder and deserving of reverence. Over their long relationship, she had listened attentively when Rosie turned to her during difficult times. She had been with her mistress during those marital roller-coaster rides, and had become quite savvy about her own supportive role.

"The bottom line is no one has ever dumped me and *lived*. Death is the easy way out. I can dish out far tougher punishment than that. I'm drawing out the pain for Sky and I'll drop two big ones next week. A one-two knockout punch. Let's see what that skinny, redheaded bitch thinks of him after he slinks off the island." Instinctively, Mango knew to open her eyes wide; she knew by the caustic tone that she would soon have to add her own vocalization. Her guardian needed comfort.

Mango hated heights, but there was a moment in her youth when she climbed a tall mango tree and swatted down a fat ripe one. Before the acrophobic tabby clawed back down, she was christened Mango. Lately, her highest trek was the sofa's summit, where she could observe most of the action in the two bedroom Ma'alaea condo.

The mango huntress had witnessed all the intimate moments in Rosie' bedroom, and had tried to understand the carnal screams that made her so jittery. She was also there for the turbulent Brahma rides with Fredrick, Rosie's second husband. It was so peaceful in the early days, and then so damn noisy during the loud arguments. All shrill noise sounded the same to her; all of it was frightening. After Fredrick disappeared and it was just the two of them, the condo was strangely silent again.

The same pattern followed for Roger and Sky. Mango never liked Roger and felt nervous around him, although his disappearance brought an end to her game of inflicting "accidental scratches." Happily for her, it had taken Roger awhile to catch on to her painful antics during their playtime. On the other hand, she missed Sky and would have snuggled up to him in a Maui minute.

"You know that bastard Fredrick deserved my 'plant blend!' The nohomalie seeds and cassava roots were ground up OK, but I should have added more Copelandia mushrooms. It was hard to know from those hamster tryouts." While Rosie ranted, Mango changed her posture and expression to show a greater look of concern. Not one whisker moved.

"The timing turned out OK, thanks to that sand truck turning onto Kihei Road. A squirt into his daily Starbuck's drink while he took a leak at Safeway couldn't have been easier. Men's habits make it way too simple. I can't believe he didn't run into a tree before swerving into that truck. Although ... getting buried in sand — how appropriate." Rosie paused for a moment and deliberately drew in a long breath. The deep inhalation fortified her mood and recharged her batteries.

Normally aloof, Mango remained steadfast during Rosie's diatribes. Draped above Rosie's head on the top of the floral-patterned sofa, she listened to the barrage of bitterness. Mango was there for the duration; she was determined not to nod off.

"I told you I could have given Roger the Rat a dose of poison anytime I wanted. He was lucky he never rejected me, and I was the one who gave him the old heave ho. But I guess he wasn't too lucky in that kayak. That was strange. Betty didn't deserve that, but what the hell do I care?" Mango nuzzled Rosie's neck and purred. She knew it was time for interaction. Her purring became louder.

"Rejecting me was the stupidest thing Sky could have done. I saw it coming, and at least I got in a few punches. Now, time is on *my* side. I still have one of his house keys. If my one-two punch doesn't drive him off this island, he'll get a chance to taste my 'medicine.' I'll add a couple more mushrooms just to be safe."

Mango knew that being Rosie's life companion required loyalty, in spite of her emotional outbursts. She turned her fluffy head and looked at the living room wall, which featured a huge three-paneled mirror across the entire length. Most of the mirror reflected the dark blue water of the Ma'alaea Bay, but the last panel of the mirror captured the reflection of Mango draped over Rosie's shoulder.

While the ocean image was alive with whitecaps and distant islands, Rosie's reflection was as scary as a water twister approaching on a direct bead. Her eyes had narrowed and become even darker than normal. The thick anger lines on her face seemed to slash wildly across her forehead. Mango turned back to her again, but her purring had ceased.

"Baby, it'll be all right. Let me brush your hair, and then I've got to look for those African necklaces. I need Liz for the knockout punch. There's no other choice. Anyway, what are friends for?" Mango stretched, crawled down into Rosie's lap, and prepared for a long period of tender grooming.

"You're the lucky one, getting your strokes all week long. I have to wait until Thursday for my quickie with Gabe. God, I'm crazy about that man. Someday, baby, someday. Then the three of us will finally be together."

Mango purred. The softer voice relaxed her.

SPIRIT OF THE FISHPOND

The Moloka'i Princess pulled out of Lahaina harbor at the crack of dawn. Sky and Gabe decided to watch the Westside morning evolve from the top deck of the ferry, which meant wiping the dew off a couple of plastic chairs. They were quickly rewarded as the sun warmed the mountain peaks above Lahaina with streaks of pink light.

"That valley Hawaiians call mother's womb," said Gabe, admiring the sunrise.

"Yeah. Most afternoons there's a rainbow over there. Those colors have given me a lot of inspiration over the years, but that dark valley *is not* on my hiking list."

The ferry served both locals and day-trippers with service to Moloka'i. To make the 45-minute crossing more interesting the captain gave a fascinating talk on Hawaiian maritime history, leading to a quiz on the return trip. Cans of beer were tossed to those with the winning answers. Sky and Gabe took the ferry every month to help the locals on Moloka'i restore one of their many fishponds. Every month they won a beer or two on the trip back.

This morning, "Captain Magellan" chose the scenic route, hugging the classy Ka'anapali coast before crossing the choppy Pailolo Channel. Alert passengers were often treated to spinner dolphins, flying fish, and occasionally flying hihimanu, the spotted eagle ray.

Once they reached the south coast of Moloka'i, the ferry passed miles of ancient fishponds — all abandoned.

"You think we'll ever see a successful year for one of those ponds?" asked Sky.

"Cannot say no mo'," Gabe replied. "Maybe sometin' we missin'. We gotta worry 'bout next winter wit' all the storms. Maybe we need change our t'inkin'. Try doin' t'ings odda way."

Gabe had been on a fishpond revitalization mission for a couple of years, and was one of the activists pushing through the snarl of state permits needed to start the rebuilding of the Maui pond at Kalepolepo. Today, the 50-acre Waialua fishpond on the south coast of Moloka'i offered an opportunity to learn the skills needed in restoring an ancient pond to full production.

Manu was waiting at Kaunakakai Wharf for them. His burly face lit up with an ear-to-ear smile.

"Aloha."

"Mornin', Manu."

Manu was one of the dedicated pond builders, as long as he was between girlfriends. His heavy-lifting energy deferred to the ancient wisdom of making hay while the sun shines, particularly when he was reaping the bounty of a wahine.

He led the Maui men to the parking lot, where his bright-maroon, monster truck was gleaming in the sun. Sky and Gabe climbed aboard, high above the 36-inch tires and the roar of the souped-up engine.

Eh, Manu, way betta view of the island comin' up here," said Gabe. "Like sittin' top triple-decker bus."

"Yeah, can get plenty good look down at da chicks."

"Even mo' betta dey no can see you way up here," teased Gabe.

"So how is the wahine hunting?" asked Sky.

"Pua left, now I talkin' to her sista."

Sky laughed. "Sounds like you better keep your motor running."

The lofty ride to the fishpond seemed imperial, and strangely voyeuristic. Conversation had to yield to the loud rumble of the engine. Manu pulled into a sandy parking spot and switched off the racket.

The ancient pond was half restored. There were hundreds of large lava rocks and thousands of smaller wedge-rocks scattered on the bottom, each waiting to be placed into the perfect niche. Sky headed into the pond anticipating another grueling, waterlogged day. He would lose a layer of leg skin, but add girth to his tanned biceps.

Gabe hesitated; something made him turn around. Silently, he turned toward the thicket of kiawe trees covering the sandy knoll.

Someone was waiting in the shadows, blending into the lower trunk of the kiawe tree. Gabe felt drawn to the figure and approached cautiously. The man looked small, almost childlike. His face finally emerged from the shade of the trees. It was an ancient face, weathered from decades of exposure, or was it centuries?

Gabe looked into his eyes and felt unsettled. Those eyes were warm and brown on the surface, but there was a flash of light from deep inside. It was like the reassuring beacon from a lighthouse, guiding the seeker with truth and direction.

"Aloha," said Gabe. "Did you call me in some way?"

"I'm Alaka'i," he said slowly, pronouncing his name "Ah-lah-KAH-ee. "I would like to share something with you. Sit down."

"I'm honored. My name is Gabe Cabalo," he answered, instinctively aware he was in the presence of a spiritual, even mystical force. Gabe settled beside the ancient one and looked out toward the incomplete fishpond. His mind raced with excitement for reasons he didn't understand. The pond appeared fuzzy as if a fog had rolled in, so he focused on the moment.

"Before we understand, we must consider three lessons," stated the diminutive Hawaiian. "If we bring these simple truths to our problems, our tasks will be clear." Gabe was hanging on every word. Sometimes the words became so soft that he strained to hear, even though he was sitting at his side.

"Learn the history, both ancient and near, and use the experiences of those early islanders to solve your problems. Remember the 'aina. On an island, the land is everything. Even with this knowledge of history and your understanding of the land, you must still be pono with your tasks."

Gabe looked again toward the ocean and was unable to bring the rock walls into focus. His generation had witnessed little success and enormous frustration in rebuilding and managing the three-walled ocean fishpond found only in Hawai'i. State meddling, invasive mangroves, hurricanes, and high winter surf contributed to the problems, along with economics and lack of cultural interest.

The numerous ancient fishponds of Hawai'i

were buried in silt, seaweed, red tape, and frustration. In centuries past they had been a vibrant and effective community enterprise.

"Yes, the fishpond," said the wise one, reading Gabe's thoughts. "There is no curse, as commonly believed, given to the ponds of Moloka'i, but the proper methods have been missing for generations. May I give you guidance?"

"Of course," replied Gabe. "Our 'ohana needs learn new approach fo' restore old tradition."

The soft-spoken man with the spiritual connection to the ancient past continued to speak. "Since you are nearing the decision on where the makaha must be placed, you need to study the sea. You must spend time in 'feeling' the currents from the outside before making your decision." His voice was both soft and strong.

"The outside current must have force to wash your pond clean, but not so strong as to crash your gates. Spend time floating in the sea outside the kuapa, and learn how the water flows past your body. This is the force that must enter the gate and not harm the nursery."

Before he continued, he exhaled deeply, and Gabe could hear a howling sound coming from his lungs — as if generations of wisdom were about to burst out.

"The purpose of the pond must include a rebuilding of the ancient culture, as well as the building of a fish community. It was always the way of the Mu, and the Wa, and of course, the Menehune. It must have cultural purpose and all the people of the island need to be included or you will fail again."

Gabe wished Sky could hear this, but realized that he alone was the conduit for this guiding flow of knowledge from another time. He vowed to remember every word and tell his friend as soon as possible.

Another hour would pass as he listened to the wisdom learned from ancient civilizations. He would learn of the Menehune, those small, peaceful agrarians who could organize a hundred-thousand residents to complete a major project in a single night, benefiting the community for years to come. For a millennium there were no wars and no rulers.

He would learn how to listen to the sacred basalt rocks lying inside the fishponds, which had been passed by strong Menehune hands from atop the highest mountain. Those rocks told of an ancient island civilization, far earlier than the Mu and the Wa, who were also farmers, fishermen, and hunters. Gabe learned the secret ways of past Hawaiian cultures, and came to realize the answers to modern problems were already there, waiting to be re-discovered.

The small man with the ancient face looked toward the opening in the fishpond and said, "If you take care of the 'aina, the 'aina will take care of you."

Silence surrounded the kiawe tree as the flash of light from the ancient eyes darkened. The warm brown eyes of Alaka'i closed. Gabe was preoccupied with processing the soft words and wise counsel, when suddenly he felt a chill and became aware of the stillness. It was time to get up and rejoin his 'ohana.

Gabe started to leave, but a wrinkled, skeletal-like arm reached out. Frozen, he watched as a weathered hand halted in front of his chest. The palm rotated and cupped toward him, suspended from another time. He felt its healing power.

Soothing words, like whispers, drifted out of lips that were nearly sealed. "*There is something more.*

The shark that you faced was a messenger bringing guidance. It was the Black Shark."

Gabe was alarmed that Alaka'i knew about his encounter with the shark, but chose to remain quiet. He knew the Hawaiian legend of the shark-god, protector of the fishpond. He had assumed the attack on him was from a rare renegade shark. Gabe shivered as he thought about the Black Shark delivering a message. He remembered the unusual black marking across its snub nose. Maybe the attack had been personal.

"Once in a great while, one must abandon his own passive nature to confront an evil. For you, the time is now. Act with your instincts, not through your character. Remember the way you confronted the Black Shark. Now is also the time for your friend to understand this. Pass these personal words to him. If you heed my teachings about the fishpond, the Black Shark will become your protector rather than your enemy." For the first time Gabe could clearly see the fishpond.

There were no formal goodbyes. Gabe felt like he had a tsunami wave of information poured over him in one great wash of enlightenment. He couldn't remember the little man leaving, or if he even said goodbye. He couldn't remember if he expressed his gratitude. As he turned around, the kiawe knoll faded as if a haze had blown in from the sea.

"I wondered where you disappeared to," said Sky. He knew Gabe rarely took a break from the heavy lifting, until it was time to run into town for a plate of chow fun. Seeing the glaze over his eyes, Sky realized that Gabe had undergone some type of transformation.

He listened throughout the day as Gabe talked

of a spiritual approach to building a fishpond, and heard details on how many sluice gates should be added, and how far the seaward rock wall should be tapered toward the ocean. He heard how to bring in a fresh stream from the mountain to make brackish water for the fish to be joyful. Clearest of all, were the personal words meant for him. The whispered words, passed through ancient lips, were clearly understood.

It was almost time for them to climb the stairs leading to the "wahine watchtower" at the top of Manu's monster truck and rumble back to the wharf. Gabe called a meeting of the 'ohana and presented his insights. Over the next few months, new thinking would change the course of rebuilding the Waialua community fishponds. A few believers would "feel the currents," after many hours of floating.

On the ride to the wharf, Sky announced, "I'm going to ask Karina to move in with me."

"'Bout time."

Sky realized his relationship with Karina was on a far higher level than he had ever known before, and was surprised that he felt completely safe in trusting her. It was time to protect that relationship — it was also time to deal directly with Rosie's vindictive cruelty.

FERRY TO THE FUTURE

On the ferry ride home, the pond builders won their beers after Captain Magellan fired off the first two questions.

"These questions get harder every month," complained Sky.

"I was t'inkin' 'bout the words of Alaka'i," said Gabe.

"Yeah, it's a lot to digest in a single gulp."

They marveled at the power of the Hawaiian Islands. The power to take a single coral polyp and build it into the underwater island of Lo'ihi off the southeast coast of the Big Island, bursting with volcanic growth from thousands of monthly quakes, and rambunctious enough to eventually become the highest mountain on the planet.

They pondered the "power of the polyp" and the island's magisterial control. Ultimately, these islands had the power to wash away the mistakes of the inhabitants through wind, fire, and flood. Fortunately, after a "cleansing," the Hawaiian Islands welcomed rebirthing, rejuvenation, and reincarnation. Warm, spiritual winds had blown across the shores of paradise for ages.

"We neva goin' get enough answers, but maybe

we learn mo' when connected to the land," said Gabe. "I try share this knowledge wit' others. Your paintings of the sea, my friend, give you special connection wit' the islands."

"As a farmer and fisherman, you even have a stronger connection," said Sky. "Now I'm really confident we can make the fishpond a success. The community needs this ancient link."

They both turned to thoughts of their personal lives. Silently, they organized a new approach to old thinking and formulated new plans as the Lahaina harbor came into view. They looked back and watched as a double silver-lining brilliantly illuminated both the top and bottom edge of a long fish-like cloud that floated over the horizon. Sheets of silver-white sunrays were sent in opposite directions from the cloud.

"Seems appropriate," said Sky.

"Yeah. Last week I watch one double green flash. First time see double. Was all cloudy on the horizon 'cept one small puka. A green flash from the sun shot above and below the puka jus' 'fore the sun get pau wit' the day."

Gabe lived in the small burg of Waikapu and spent most his time managing his large pig farm. He was isolated from island gossip and Rosie's rumors. His friendship with Sky had never included conversation about Rosie.

"How's Angelina?" asked Sky.

"Same, but now everythin' 'bout for change."

Gabe thought about his wife and then Rosie. He knew it was time to break off the weekly affair with Rosie. Right now, he felt strong enough to deal with Rosie's rage and her threats of retaliation.

The affair had started six months after her breakup with Sky, and he remembered how soft she was in the beginning. At church meetings, she had seemed so virtuous, and so in need of a man's touch. Later, the threat of her blackmail overshadowed his carnal desire, which had been heightened by having an unresponsive wife.

Angelina had lived with her own torment for years, incapable of making love or demonstrating affection toward Gabe. She loved Gabe, but was a prisoner to the power of booze.

"Hope those surfers clear before we ride the waves into the harbor," said Sky.

"Hmmm." Gabe was deep in thought. Three months ago, Rosie had given Gabe a bottle of medicine that she claimed would take care of Angelina's problem, once and for all. She told him that it would have a dramatic effect and should be used only as a last resort.

Gabe never considered giving Angelina the "medicine," and as time went by he forgot the bottle was still hidden in his garage. Thinking about how scary Rosie had become, he vowed to dump the bottle tonight; Thursday night after their church group he would dump Rosie. Furthermore, he felt he had a new power that would finally find the right therapy to conquer the demons that were tormenting his beautiful wife.

"Good luck," said Sky. He decided to walk over to his gallery the minute he was ashore and see if Boomer, his trusted manager, was willing to take a couple days off for some sleuth work, possibly a quick trip to Rosie's home state of Illinois. He planned to hire a detective if Boomer didn't dig up anything.

This particular day would never be forgotten by either of the pond builders; it held the rebirthing of their own two lives and the promise of rebirth for Angelina.

188

ZULU MASKS

After a jam-packed day of island activities, Sky and Karina sprawled out in the African room.

"The famous 'Sky's the Limit Mai Tais'," said Karina, as she enjoyed the sweet taste of her drink. "Special rum? Or is the ice from a succulent polar cube?"

"The secret is in the mix," replied Sky as he headed toward the barroom to prepare another batch of his tropical rum concoction. After he left the room, a muffled sound came from his direction; it sounded like "Mr. & Mrs. T mix."

Karina thought about yesterday's events. The mailman had delivered a letter from her Norwegian husband stating that all the papers were processed, and the divorce was imminent. That felt good. Then, at Safeway she bumped into Rosie's buddy, Liz, who seemed as sweet as the early morning dew dripping from a plumeria blossom. After pleasantries, Liz declared that Sky was one cool guy, but couldn't believe he stole Rosie's African necklaces.

Her words had sounded casual. "Didn't he have enough African junk? Rosie figures he's keeping them in one of his secret hiding places." She mentioned two possible locations, and then directed her skinny pole legs toward an empty cashier's aisle.

While Sky was mixing up another round of mai tais, Karina thought about how much she had fallen in love with him over these last few months, and how she had grown to trust him. Unfortunately, the same curiosity that killed the cat was killing her at the moment. She didn't believe Liz's bullshit for a minute, but then what could be the harm in searching two hiding places?

The curse of the curious feline already compelled her to paw under the first location, a giant Senegalese drum in the corner of Sky's living room. It yielded a dead cockroach, a wall of spider webs, and a trail of gecko scat.

At the moment, the male and female Zulu masks were staring down at her, driving her feline curiosity right up that wall. The African masks were imposing, primitive, and harboring enough space to hide the Queen of England's ceremonial crown. According to Liz, the masks were another likely hideaway.

"It's for your own good," Sky said on his return. "If you knew the formula, you could be tortured by a mob of tourists trying to get my secret mai tai ingredients. Tell me. What was your favorite part of the day: snorkeling with the dolphins this morning at La Perouse Bay, the lava pond picnic, or the sleepless nap this afternoon?"

"I have to admit, you sure know how to fire up the hormonal juices of a proper lady. You could have a career firing up the engines of female tourists seeking exotic-island escapades. Wait! Cancel that. You're far too busy revving up *my* motor to have any more time."

"Hey, it's kind of hard taking a nap next to a freckled Viking."

"I'll say it's hard! But to answer your question, while nothing can top a nap with my safari guide; my heart went out to those two baby dolphins swimming with their protective pod. Snorkeling with those dolphins made my heart flutter."

"That pod has been circling swimmers for years," said Sky. "Sometimes they don't show up if too many boats or people are in the water. I believe they're picky about who they want to entertain. Did you notice the two flankers at the outside edge of the pod, watching us every second?"

"I did!"

"What about the lava pond?"

"So it's definitely brackish water out there in the middle of that lava bed? Where's it come from?"

"The salt water comes from underground lava tubes connecting the pond with the ocean. The freshwater must come from rain, although it's always been another mystery for me. Think of it as our private little fishpond. You have to enjoy the mysteries on Maui and try not to understand everything. Looks like you're ready for another round of my famous mai tais."

"I want a little umbrella this time," said Karina, hoping the extra search might give her enough time to lift up those big Zulu masks. She suspected that Liz was a fool, but there was only one way to prove it. She had to peek.

Sky grabbed the empty glasses, gave Karina a tender kiss on her forehead, and left for the barroom.

Karina quickly approached the primitive male mask, hanging from two large hooks. She pulled back the chin and peeked underneath. Nothing! She listened for Sky and heard him rustling around the bar area. Maybe there was time to check out the

191

female — it was now or never. The second she pulled back on the primitive chin, three beautiful necklaces dropped to the floor. Karina was aghast!

She grabbed them and rushed toward her purse, all the while watching for Sky's return. She heard footsteps as she stuffed the necklaces inside her purse. Looking back toward the female mask, she panicked. It was horribly askew!

"Angel, do me a special favor," she said, trying to recover and look playful at the same time. "Bring me a maraschino cherry. Just this once." Sky gave her a funny look, smiled, and turned around. When he returned to the living room, the Zulu wall appeared normal.

Tired from their physical day, they decided to watch a DVD on the home theater screen.

During the movie, Karina tried to understand how the necklaces could have been there. She guessed they were Rosie's missing necklaces, and she suspected that Rosie planted them, using her spare key to Sky's place. She was absolutely sure of one thing; she would not mention this to anyone. She knew everything would be explained in time.

Karina gave Sky a kiss that would ring his chimes for some time to come and then said. "Love you. I'm totally exhausted, let's crash."

"Love you back. What a great day."

"Yeah, it was completely surreal."

In two hours, the clocks on the mainland would do their October ritual and "fall back." On Maui, a lot was changing, but time stood still.

SCANDAL IN LAHAINA

A storm of scandal roared into Lahaina on Monday. The second part of Rosie's one-two punch had been delivered and was quickly turning into the biggest art scandal in Hawaiian memory.

At 11 a.m., Wailea socialite Elizabeth Brinkley called the Whaler's Weekly, a local Lahaina rag. She reported that two Sky Shafer sea life "originals" were appraised in Honolulu and discovered to be fraudulent copies, noting the difference between a Shafer original and a reproduction was a whopping $75,000. She announced that she was suing Shafer Galleries, and the readers of their newspaper should be forewarned.

By 2 p.m., two of Sky's clients, tipped off by Rosie Faber, called the same publication. They were outraged that their sea life "originals," signed by Sky Shafer, were only run of the mill lithographs. Furthermore, their attorneys would be seeking the return of their money, plus punitive damages. The gusts of accusations blowing through Lahaina had increased to a category-three storm.

An hour later, two Maui radio stations called the Whaler's Weekly. They wanted confirmation that the weekly was about to expose fraudulent art galleries in a special edition set for Tuesday afternoon. The Lahaina rag confirmed they were working on the story.

In truth, they only had one ace reporter, currently on vacation in Las Vegas, and three part-time reporters. Bobbie Jones, the restaurant critic, who had never reviewed a cuisine or eatery that she hadn't adored, got the assignment.

Art galleries in Lahaina were big business. Ms. Jones was skilled in reporting new restaurant openings, sudden closings, and the reshuffling of sous-chefs throughout the island. She had never confronted a hurricane of scandal ripping through the reputation of renowned Lahaina art galleries.

Taking the day off from the animal shelter, Rosie made calls from her home. She contacted every important art client living in Hawai'i whom she could remember from her days living with Sky.

Liz personally knew two socialites who owned a Shafer original and buzzed them with an "early warning" alert. By evening, the scandal raging through the phone lines of Bobbie Jones' office had escalated to a category four.

On Tuesday morning, every media outlet in the state tried to get the story from the editor of the Whaler's Weekly. He announced that he would fax a summary to everyone just before the special edition hit the streets; the ETA was for 3 p.m. It would become the lead news story in Hawai'i that evening on radio and television.

By the next day, the fraudulent art story reached the strength of a devastating hurricane. Art patrons throughout the state reevaluated their investments; the wealthy ones contacted their legal representatives. Panic blew through every art gallery in the state, focusing on the Shafer Galleries and the Planet Galleries; both had branches in Honolulu and Kona.

Sky fumed, but remained confident that his battle plan was sound. In the evening, he called Karina to reassure her, relaying his strategy.

"She's a fraud! Boomer contacted the College of Veterinary Medicine in Illinois. They said Rosie had a great record, high scores, and perfect attendance. But she dropped out the last year. She never received any credentials!"

"Be careful, sweetie. She could be dangerous."

"I'll deal with her later, but now I'm bringing this scandal to a quick halt. I've scheduled a news conference for tomorrow morning.

"What will you say?"

"Honey, you won't even recognize me. I'm taking this battle head-on; I'll make just two announcements.

"I hired two independent appraisers from Oahu and three more are flying in from California to be available to any patron of mine who requests an appraisal for originality and authenticity at no cost to them.

"I'm also announcing that I have become aware of the two perpetrators of the scandal, and my team of attorneys will be filing criminal charges within 48 hours."

"Good for you. Sometimes we have to step out of our box to protect ourselves. I've never doubted your integrity. You'll clear up this mess."

"Thanks. I have to go now. Goodnight. Love you."

"Love you, too." She decided it was time to anonymously drop Rosie's necklaces off at the Faber

Animal Shelter.

Thursday afternoon, after Sky's forceful public statements, the focus switched to one chain called Planet Galleries, owned by a large mainland corporation. They represented artists from all over the country; selling originals had been a large part of their success.

While many of Sky's patrons made public statements in his support, three independent art appraisers from Oahu announced that Sky's originals were indeed authentic. But they discovered that a number of the "originals" purchased from Planet Galleries were actually reproductions. The eye of the storm glared down on Planet Galleries for the next two months, ending in lawsuits, bankruptcy, and eviction. A tee-shirt shop eventually filled the scandalous space.

CHURCH SPY

On Thursday night Sky looked at his bleeding arm and silently cursed. He had been waiting outside the rear meeting room of the Waikapu Unity Church, hidden behind a thorny bougainvillea hedge. While parting the brambly bush for a better view, the branches had snapped free and ripped his skin.

As he listened to the chatter of the church group, Rosie's voice clearly dominated the conversations; the topics included far more island gossip than biblical examination. The meeting seemed to be breaking up and it wasn't clear if Gabe was there. Sky tried to make himself as invisible as the white flies, which were curling the leaves of the purple shrub.

The first one out the rear door was Gabe, and he appeared to be in a hurry. Still chatting with her friends, Rosie left in the last group. Sky walked cautiously through the rear yard to his rented Nissan, parked a short distance away on a side street near Honoapi'ilani Highway. It would be easy to spot the small Miata driving past his stakeout.

A few minutes later, Rosie drove slowly past him on the highway. Sky followed at a distance and was astonished to see her turn into the narrow, rutted lane leading to Gabe's pig farm. He parked the rental car and noticed he was still bleeding from the scratches. Cleaning up the driver's seat would have to be postponed. Right now he had to confirm his suspicions about Rosie and Gabe. Nothing would surprise him anymore regarding Rosie — but Gabe?

It had been a long time since he had visited Gabe on his farm and shared a beer in the office. The lane leading to the office was pitch black, and the ruts made his espionage work dangerous. Already, he had tumbled twice. His anger increased each time he picked himself up.

He knew he had become the target, once more, of a woman's fury. This time he vowed it would be different. He couldn't let his life be destroyed again. He was prepared to confront this harassment and end it once and for all. His forehead tightened so much that it hurt. He didn't care anymore; he wanted his life back.

It had been 20 years since he had felt this much anger. He remembered being pummeled while attempting to rescue the demented woman who then turned against him. The bitterness over those lost years further ignited his anger. He picked up the pace toward Gabe's office.

Then he thought about his buddy. How could Gabe not only betray their close friendship, but betray his wife?

He smelled the pigs well before he saw the faint glow of light, then he heard them rutting around the muck. Hundreds of them were grunting and snorting.

Standing before the rundown building, he realized his battle plan was fuzzy. He gently stretched his long legs over the creaky wood steps and stepped up to the window. Unconsciously, he clenched both hands, thinking how easy it would be to break down the dilapidated paper-thin door.

The farm office had a large sofa and mini-bar, and by pig-farm standards there were plenty of creature comforts. The small window on the door was coated with dirt, making it nearly impossible to see through. The single 60-watt bulb inside the office offered little help.

Despite the lack of illumination, he could see Rosie sitting on the sofa, naked from the waist up. Her large, perky breasts were aimed directly at Gabe, standing in the center of the room. In spite of the seductive weapons pointing at him, Gabe stood nervously in the room with his arms folded. His angry words were quick and far louder than necessary, easily penetrating the thin wall. Sky felt like he was standing inside.

"It's over," shouted Gabe. "Plenty stupid, screwin' 'round wit' you! No mo' you threaten me. Over 'tween us. You need go home! *Go home!*"

Sky spun around and ran to the car, ignoring the rough road. Strangely, he felt compassion for his friend. There was no need for physical confrontation. The dark, combative period in his life was long ago. When he reached his car phone, he pressed Gabe's number.

"What?"

"It's Sky."

"Jesus, Sky, plenty late! I thought somethin' maybe 'bout my kids. What the hell's up?"

"I'll be quick. I know you're having an affair and risking humiliation for your family." He paused so that Gabe could prepare for more of his rapid-fire accusations.

"I want you to tell Rosie right now that I know about the affair. Tell her that she will be presented with a criminal lawsuit for her art-fraud accusations, and every state agency will soon know that she's practicing without a veterinary license. They can decide how to prosecute her. Good luck, Gabe. I mean it. I hope we'll still be friends." Sky slapped the cell phone shut.

ROAD RAGE

Stepping into the tropical night, Rosie felt as angry as she had ever been. Nobody dumps me and gets away with it, she thought. Gabe, the only man she ever loved unconditionally — and the man she planned to share the rest of her life — just dumped her. Now the entire year with him seemed wasted.

She had never seen that intense look in Gabe's eyes before. His words were sharp and final. For the first time in their relationship she knew she had no choice but to comply. To hell with him, she thought.

She realized that Sky not only knew about the affair, but more importantly knew about her phony vet credentials. She was furious that she hadn't gotten the satisfaction of seeing Sky crumble from her elaborate scheme.

"Damn it! I knew better!" she mumbled as she approached her car. "Should have poisoned him a long time ago. It would have been so damn easy."

She knew that she would miss the quickies with Gabe. At least it was the last time she would have to listen to the grunts of those damn pigs, although the noise gave cover to her own cries of pleasure. Her anger continued to build as she turned the ignition.

As she guided her topless Miata onto Honoapi'ilani Highway, her anger turned to rage. She tightened the grip on the steering wheel as tears clouded her vision. In the darkened night the concrete walls over the 1937 Waikapu Bridge were vague. Rosie jerked her head up and brushed back the tears just in time to steer her Miata away from the walls and down the deserted highway.

She knew her life on Maui was over, and wondered if Sky suspected that she was a murderess. She couldn't imagine the humiliation of a trial.

Rosie drove past a long row of yellow-flowered trees, flourishing along the south side of the highway. She recalled collecting seedpods from those poisonous plants years ago. They were the most effective ingredients in her lethal "medicinal drinks."

The Tropical Plantation came into view on the opposite side of the road. Her heart pounded, but strangely she flashed on the time she took the miniature-train ride through the pineapple field with Fredrick, her second husband. Or was he her third?

Rosie picked up speed, and the cool breezes helped dry her face. She realized that she could never again be a veterinarian, and that she would be the laughing stock of the island because of her affair with Gabe. It was all too much.

The Miata weaved back and forth across the center of the highway, but the road was still deserted. Far off in the distance a truck could be seen coming from Ma'alaea. She picked up speed. Ahead, monkeypod and royal poinciana trees canopied over the highway. Two of the thick, hard trunks sheltered little white crosses — fatality crosses. Fresh flowers had been lovingly placed at the base of the roadside memorials.

"Why the hell did I give Gabe that bottle of poison?" she shouted into the dark night. "My God, what if he still has it! Men are so stupid."

Further down, her sports car zipped over the small rise in the highway. The truck came closer. Her heart skipped a beat — it was a tractor-trailer rig. A flood of frightening memories washed over her. She raced past a series of enormous metal power poles, gaining speed on the downhill stretch. Her entire body quivered as she passed the truck.

Rosie was losing control. The last year of hopes and dreams with Gabe were shattered, along with her social and professional life. Her heart-rate skyrocketed north, and her motor skills plummeted south. Luckily, the road was empty as another wave of rage took over.

"Shit," she yelled. "I'm not going home!" She suddenly felt compelled to drive to Liz's house and tell her everything. She looked at the construction lights ahead, blinking a warning for the upcoming, reconfigured intersection.

She spun the steering wheel left toward Wailea. The car crossed the centerline and left the highway, barely missing a thick power pole. She was shocked at how fast she was going.

"Where the hell is the...."

The Miata shot across the thick grass just a few yards before the intersection of flashing yellow signs. At 70 miles an hour and not one obstacle in the way, the car left the ground at the edge of the biggest industrial landfill pit on Maui. The small vehicle flew straight across the center of the pit, hovering 25 feet above the gigantic canyon, before gravity reached up and pulled it down into piles of loose organic fill and industrial waste.

Once the black convertible darted off the road and sailed into the landfill, it became invisible. The giant pit was totally dark.

The car landed on tons of kiawe branches dumped that afternoon from a large overgrown parcel. The branches split apart and gave way as tons of metal crashed through the forest of cut wood. The car dropped through the debris, nearly out of sight. Rosie died on impact.

A smoldering fire, burning for six weeks in the bowels of the pit, had ended only the week before — and had left a void beneath the surface. Since then, the landfill company had not risked running heavy equipment over the center area. Compaction was too dangerous until more rocks and dirt could be added.

A few moments later the car settled further into the organic waste; even the top of the windshield disappeared. The idling engine coughed and died. Finally, a few roadside crickets broke the dead silence. A car hummed along the highway.

GREAT STORM

The south-coast skies that reach far past the islands of Kahoʻolawe and Lanaʻi into the "great beyond" usually appear in warm, reassuring shades of blue. On occasion, they change into a light, hazy gray. Islanders understand the reasons.

Residents know that the strong Kona winds of the Big Island sometimes blow vog from the erupting volcano, Kilauea, across the channel to Maui. They smell it. They also recognize the burning smell from a torched cane field before the cane is harvested. They can visually track the drifting gray clouds of ash heading out to sea. Both sights are familiar.

On Friday morning the skies were dark gray, bordering on black. The air was still with faint hope of a breeze. Without light, the waters off the south coast had the same blackened color. The rare daytime darkness started near the shoreline and reached into the "great beyond."

Old timers sensed the ominous nature of the looming storm. The unusual sight of the black ocean, the black sky, and the missing horizon terrified some of them. The thick, sticky air added to their fears.

Friday was a holiday, but not for everyone.

Employees at the Faber Animal Shelter had the day off. The landfill in Maʻalaea was open for business.

By noon, nine truckloads of rock were dumped into the middle of the commercial pit. Then the rain came. The rain was gentle, but steady. By two p.m., the manager locked the gates, worried that a big rig would get stuck in the mud.

In 1871, Maui experienced the so-called "hundred-year flood." Since then, Maʻalaea and Kihei averaged less than 15 inches of rain a year, mostly in the winter. Most desert areas are ill-prepared for a deluge of rain; South Maui was no exception.

The National Weather Service predicted a good soaker for all the Hawaiian Islands on Friday, then clearing, returning to typical 10 to 20 MPH westerlies on Saturday. The low-pressure trough swept warm, wet, southerly air across all the islands, but the eye of the storm favored Maui. The weather service had no way of knowing that the storm would stall.

By Saturday morning more than five inches of rain dumped on South Maui. The Pacific Disaster Center also responded with a bulletin that predicted the center of the storm would blow away from the island in the afternoon.

It did, but then it circled around and returned like a vengeful bully. It squatted over the island and pissed like it had been holding its bladder for over a hundred years. The flood of water roaring down Haleakala and the West Maui Mountains joined forces with the rivers of mud in the central valley and aimed its ugly discharge toward the ocean. The fury lasted all weekend; some gauges recorded the equivalent of two years of rain.

"I'm running out of rain jokes," said Karina.

"It's no longer funny," said Sky. "At least my house seems to be holding up OK. No leaks in the roof, but the doors are a mess."

"Thank God we're together. I can't imagine the problems that some people are having. Your house is high enough, and the drainage in Wailea seems to be holding. Don't worry."

"I won't," he said, giving her a strong hug and a gentle kiss.

Few islanders made it to work on Monday. Roads were flooded and most were still closed on Tuesday. Ma'alaea Bay was churning with high surf and powerful, reddish-brown waves. It was the catch basin for anything not firmly attached. For the first time in memory, surfers stayed home as the bay was filled with outdoor furniture, cars, palm trees, and unimaginable junk.

Eleven people were reported missing. Later, three washed ashore and three more were discovered holed up in an upcountry bar. The fate of five people would never be known.

On Wednesday, the roads were clear for traffic again. The staff at the Faber Animal Shelter reported Rosie missing, worried that she had been swept out to sea in her car.

Three weeks later, there was a memorial at sea for Rosie Faber. It took place outside the harbor, directly in front of her condo. Half of the harbor boats paid tribute, and folks came from all over the island to pay their respects. In the eyes of the community, as well as her glorification by the press, she represented the human side of the tragedy caused by the hundred-year storm. Eulogies filled the gentle air above the sea. Sky and Gabe stayed home and chose silence. The island had spoken.

QUEEN'S THRONE

Water tumbled 200 feet into the pool of Makahiku Falls, causing vapor to rise beyond the top of the cataract. It was late in December, and the four hikers watched the spectacle from the cliff's edge. This was their first scenic stop on the trail to the "Queens Throne."

"I'm so glad you guys could join us," said Karina to Buddy and Joni. Buddy was sitting on a small stump with Joni in his lap. He held her tight; his hefty arms wrapped around her waist while his chin rested on her left shoulder.

"Yeah, good friends and waterfalls," said Sky. "Nice combo."

"I brought soap for a shower under the waterfall," said Joni.

"No soap in da streams, baby," said Buddy.

"The jet action beats a deluxe spa any day," said Sky.

"Not as warm though," said Karina.

"True, but you don't need to clean the filters. Remember to ease into it or you'll be pulverized."

Until recently, the pools of Oheo were called the Seven Sacred Pools. The former name had a nice ring to it, and the tourist industry kept the name alive for decades to draw visitors to the area. But, as the Hawaiian community pointed out, the remote pools at Kipahulu were never sacred, and there were a lot more than seven.

Powerful and gentle views of plummeting water were abundant at the vista points to Waimoku Falls. The two-hour hike offered a large variety of other fascinations, making it the most diverse hike in the Hawaiian Islands. Their morning destination was the secret sister of the massive, 400-foot Waimoku Falls.

"Gabe told me the 'great storm' opened up a wider path to the Queen's Throne," said Sky. "In the past, we had to walk up the middle of the stream and crawl over the boulders. Then we had to rope our way up the side of a series of waterfalls. Not exactly a walk in the park."

"Speaking of Gabe," said Karina. "Angelina is officially two months dry."

"That's wonderful!" exclaimed Joni. "How did she manage that?"

"Gabe told her that she wouldn't be left alone until she was completely well. He stayed with her for a week before he called a couple of friends, including Sky and myself.

"I'm part of a six-woman support team. We stay with her when Gabe's not there. I think she'll be fine — and she's so beautiful. I never noticed her peppy personality before."

"Good for you guys," said Buddy. "At least dey stay in love dat whole time. I bet da kids happy."

"Yeah, they deserve the best, and I like my small part. She's back with AA too."

"I can help," said Joni. "Call me when you need another volunteer."

"Thanks, I will," said Karina. She thought about

her own life and last month's dramatic events.

The day after her divorce was finalized and all the papers were sitting on her desk, Sky asked her to move in with him. She would tell him soon about his wonderful timing. Right now she was trying to control her emotions. Sky had carefully billed this hike as an extraordinary event in their lives — a pivotal moment. She was convinced that he was carrying a ring in his pocket, and she couldn't wait to accept his proposal. She had never felt so ready.

"Ready to wander through the bamboo jungle?" asked Sky.

"You first go," said Buddy.

They passed banyan trees, wide and embracing, like the spirit of aloha. Hundreds of Tarzan vines dangled to the ground from the fat horizontal branches. Bird's nest ferns found comfort in the nurturing crotch of jungle trees. Giant elephant-ear taro grew wild in ancient fields, and moisture-loving green ti plants reached for the sky. They passed through meadows and jungles, and forests of ripe guava and passion fruit, before the lime-green tops of a young bamboo forest came into view.

They walked through the yellow-tubed saplings and entered into the kingdom of stately old-growth bamboo. The towering plants proliferated into a dense jungle, making passage impossible without a machete-wielding guide.

Years ago, the National Park Service opened a path through the center of the forest and a boardwalk lifted hikers over the muddy areas. Scant light penetrated all the way down to the damp forest floor. A profusion of noise reverberated through the forest.

"I do *not* want to be here in the middle of the night," said Joni. "It sounds like the tops are breaking off."

A strong wind whipped the tops of the hollow skinny poles, creating a chorus of beating sticks. The trunks rubbed against each other, sounding like the drunken groans from the losers in a barroom brawl.

"No worry, dey plenty strong," said Buddy. "Dey survived da 'great storm,' not like odda stuff on dis island. Neva did find dem cars. Dey still be missin' five people, includin' Rosie. I'll bet you neva t'ink your ole girlfriend goin' be da local martyr?"

"Go figure," said Sky. "The community needed to heal after all that damage. Rosie represented a rallying figure for all kinds of causes. They're raising lots of money in her name."

"Everyone can relate to a lack of closure," said Karina. "God bless her." She guessed that Rosie had a key to Sky's house, and wondered if she had tossed that centipede through the front door at some odd hour. It would have been easy.

"I know she also had a dark side," said Joni. "I wouldn't be surprised if she came back as a shark."

"I t'ink one cockroach," said Buddy. "Speakin' of bugs, I hear dat Gecko adopted Rosie's cat."

"She loves cats," said Sky. "Mango will get the royal treatment. There's the first bridge. Remember, ole pal, when we had to wade across the stream?"

"Yeah, dat not long ago. I seen dis stream look like one big river wit' couple hours rain. Crossin' it plenty fun. Now challenge no mo'."

"This bridge was built for us normal people," said Joni, "and the view down the gorge is awesome."

"But dey no figure on da crazies jumpin' off it," said Buddy. "Eh, Karina, how's da whale watch last week?"

"Like a reunion with your favorite friends. We saw a mother and her yearling."

"There was breaching in the distance," said Sky, "but the rest of the whales should be here next month. The tourists and the humpbacks are gathering for a brand new season."

After they left the bridge, they walked in silence listening to the clacking sticks of the bamboo, the playful songs of two Japanese quail, and the melody of an amorous pair of Norther cardinals. The swooshing sound of distant waterfalls became louder. They stopped at the last side stream before Waimoku Falls. It was the staging area for their assault toward the secret pool of the majestic Queen's Throne waterfall.

"No wonder it's a secret," said Karina, "nobody would notice this trail."

"What trail?" questioned Buddy. "You jus' follow da mud slide. Only da locals and rangers know 'bout it."

"Let's go," said Joni, "I'm ready to peel off all my clothes and get a shoulder massage."

"Me too," said Karina.

"It's straight up, so hang on to roots and branches," said Sky. He thought about his plan one more time. He realized that complete trust and a lifetime commitment had been a long time coming, but deep down he knew he was ready. After their swim and lunch, he would find the perfect spot in front of the Queen's Throne and kneel before Karina. Holding a diamond ring, he would talk about his love for her and ask for her hand. The words would be easy. He had never been so ready.

Thirty minutes later, they were dripping with sweat and sitting on boulders in front of the silver-white sheen of water cascading toward them. The falls welcomed them with a wide selection of nurturing therapy, fluctuating between a gentle mist spray and a pulsating shoulder massage. They left all their clothes on the rocks to dry and waded into the serene pool. It seemed like the natural thing to do on an island paradise.

GLOSSARY

ali'i — chiefs
aloha — love, greetings!
haole — Caucasian
hipahipa — cheers!
imu — underground oven
kalua — baked in an underground oven
kapu — taboo, forbidden
keiki — kids
kiawe — thorny coastal tree
koa — prized Hawaiian hardwood
kuapa — rock wall
kukui — candlenut tree, state tree
kupuna — elders
lehua — flower of the island of Hawai'i
lu'au — Hawaiian feast
mahalo — thanks
mahimahi — dolphin fish
maile — native twining shrub
makaha — sluice gate
mauka — inland/uphill
Mauna Kahalawai — West Maui Mtns.
muumuu — loose gown
mynah — Asian starling
naupaka — native shrub
'ohana — family
'ono — delicious
pali — cliff
paniolo — cowboy
pareu — sarong-type body cover
petrels — tube-nosed seabirds
poi — made from cooked taro corms
poi dog — Hawaiian mongrel
pono — harmony and goodness
puka — hole
pupu — snack
taro — stemless plant, source of poi
ti — woody plant, long flat leaves
ulua — species of jack fish
vog — volcanic ash/smog
wahine — woman

ABOUT THE AUTHOR

Rick Olson graduated with B.S. degrees in psychology, sociology, and journalism at Western Michigan University. His travels to over one hundred countries set the stage for numerous adventure stories. For the past twenty years, he has roamed the mystical places on Maui and currently resides on the south side, at the water's edge.